THE
YEAR
I FLEW
AWAY

THE YEAR I FLEW AWAY

By Marie Arnold

Versify
An Imprint of HarperCollinsPublishers

Library of Congress Cataloging-in-Publication Data

Names: Arnold, Marie, author.

Title: The year I flew away / by Marie Arnold.

Description: Boston : Houghton Mifflin Harcourt, [2021] | Audience: Ages 10 to 12. | Audience: Grades 4–6. | Summary: After moving from her home in Haiti to her uncle's home in Brooklyn, ten-year-old Gabrielle, feeling bullied and out of place, makes a misguided deal with a witch.

Identifiers: LCCN 2019036630 (print) | LCCN 2019036631 (ebook) | ISBN 9780358733331 (pbk.) | ISBN 9780358273271 (ebook)

Subjects: CYAC: Moving, Household—Fiction. | Immigrants—Fiction. | Witchcraft—Fiction. | Friendship—Fiction. | Haitian Americans—Fiction.

Classification: LCC PZ7.1.A7632 Sum 2021 (print) | LCC PZ7.1.A7632 (ebook) | DDC [Fic]—dc23

LC record available at https://lccn.loc.gov/2019036630

LC ebook record available at https://lccn.loc.gov/2019036631

Hand-lettering by Andrea Miller

Typography by Andrea Miller

22 23 24 25 26 PC/CWR 10 9 8 7 6 5 4 3 2 1

First paperback edition, 2022

For Haiti
&
the ones who struggle to belong

CHAPTER ONE
The River That Wasn't There

IT TAKES HARD WORK to eat nine mangoes back to back, but that's just what I'm going to do. I'm about to become mango champion of my village. My best friend, Stephanie, stacks a pile of mangoes in front of me. The boys assemble their stack in front of Paul, the boy I will be racing against. This match has been a long time coming. All the kids in the village put off their chores to watch us.

My heart is beating loud and fast, like a drum at a carnival. I look over at Paul. He's taller, bigger, and quicker than me. But today is not his day; it's mine. I've been practicing. I turn and nod to Stephanie; she smiles back at me. We are ready.

All the kids shout, "One, two, three—eat!"

I bite into my first mango—it tastes like honey and summer. It oozes out sticky-sweet nectar that runs down my fingers. I tear into another with my teeth, suck all the juices out, then toss the skin aside and start on a new one. While the boys laugh and make fun of me for even trying to beat Paul, I rip into my third mango.

Paul is showing off by juggling some of the mangoes before he eats them. He's so sure that he'll win that he takes time to joke around. But I'm not joking around. This is serious. I'm on my seventh mango. Soon, the boys notice that I am ahead and close to winning. That's when they call out to Paul and demand that he eat faster.

"She's a girl! You can't let her win!" the boys shout.

"Hurry, Gabrielle! Hurry!" Stephanie shouts.

Paul speeds up—he's like a hungry animal. I'm on my last mango, but Paul is close to catching up with me.

"You can do it!" The girls cheer as my victory gets closer. I bite and chew through the last mango, just as Paul is about to finish his. It's close—but not close enough. I toss aside the final mango skin, and it lands in the bucket before Paul's mango does—I win!

"Yay!" Stephanie and I rejoice with the other girls.

"Gabrielle Marie Jean, you better not be in another mango contest!" My mom's voice rings throughout the village. The crowd scatters, everyone but Stephanie.

"You better not be staining that dress, it's one of your good ones . . ." my mom says. I can't see her yet, but her voice fills up the village. She's getting closer. I look down at my dress, and it's dripping with mango juice and dirt.

"Ah, we gotta go!" I say to Stephanie as I grab her hand. We run off and head to our favorite hiding place—the crawl-space under the church. We wiggle our way inside and lie flat on our stomachs. We look out at the parade of shoes and sandals going by us.

We hear my mom asking other grownups where I am. They all tell her they don't know. My mom calls out my name. Judging by her tone, I'm really in for it.

"We can't hide here forever," Stephanie says.

"Maybe we hide just long enough for my mom to find something else to be mad about."

"Okay, but you are usually the reason she's mad, so . . ."

Stephanie's right. I am usually the one who makes my mom use her I'm-not-happy-with-you face. And yes, sometimes I do get into trouble, but it's mostly not my fault. Like, it's not my fault that I like competing against the boys. They think that because they are boys they can do everything better. So it's up to Stephanie and me to show them girls can do stuff too. Also, it's not my fault that mangoes are so good that I have to eat them all.

"Gabrielle, you have three seconds to come out from wherever you're hiding!" my mom warns as we watch her red sandals get closer. Stephanie and I look at each other with wide eyes.

"Go, save yourself," I tell her.

"I can't leave you here alone," she replies.

"It's too late for me. Go!"

"Okay. Good luck," she says as she crawls out of our hiding spot.

I hear footsteps approaching. I see red sandals head toward me and then stop. Mom knows I'm under here. But she doesn't scold me or yank me out from under the crawl-space. Instead, she sits at the base of the steps.

"Well, I can't find my daughter. I guess I better get a new one. One who doesn't get mud and mango juice all over her dress. One who finishes her chores before she goes to play. But even if this new daughter is perfect, I'll still miss the one I had before. The one who gave the best hugs and made me laugh. The daughter who almost won a mango contest."

"Almost?" I shout in disbelief. I crawl out from under the church to defend my championship. I stand before her. "Mom, I won, I really won!"

"Yes, I know," she says as she stands up.

That's when I realize . . . "Hey, you tricked me!"

"Moms are allowed to trick their kids. Now, explain yourself. You are a mess, young lady!" she says.

"I know, I'm sorry, but I had to compete."

She looks me over, but this time she twists her lips from side to side. I think that means she's thinking.

"Am I in trouble?" I ask.

"Well, that depends. Who did you beat out to win the mango contest?"

"Paul."

"He's twice your size!" she says with a big grin. She quickly changes her expression, like she just remembered she was supposed to be upset. "You should be grounded this evening. Which is a shame, because guess whose bones have been talking?"

"Madame Tita?" I ask as I start jumping up and down.

Madame Tita is a round woman with pretty skin, like midnight. She wears colorful wraps on her head and moves like a turtle. Her voice is deep and rumbles. She sounds like what mountains would sound like if mountains had a voice. She's one hundred years old, and what she says goes because she's the oldest. When her bones ache a little, she says they're talking to her. And when her bones speak, it usually means it's going to rain!

Rain is even better than mangoes. When it rains, it's playtime for us kids. The adults have to work by gathering the water and storing it to use later. And here's the best part— our parents let us play, jump, and dance in the rain. That way, we get clean without having to use the water they saved up.

"Madame Tita said it's going to rain?" I ask.

"Yes. Her bones have spoken; rain will come soon. I'll let you play in it, but only if you promise no more mango contests."

"But Mom . . ."

She places her hands on her hips and tilts her head to the side. Uh-oh, head tilting is never good.

"You have to make a decision. Rain or mangoes?" she says.

"Rain."

She smiles. "I had a feeling you'd say that."

"Mom, I worked really hard to win today. And I did. So, if I work hard to get something, does that mean I will always get it?" I ask.

She bends down so that our eyes meet, and she moves one of my braids away from my face. "Gabrielle, if you work hard and do your best, there's nothing you can't do."

"Can I fly a plane?"

"Yes, you can do that."

"How?"

"Well, first you have to go to school to learn all about planes."

Something makes my heart hurt, and I hold on to my chest and look down at the ground.

"What is it, Ba-Ba?" my mom asks, calling me by my nickname.

"We don't have money to send me to airplane school."

"Gabrielle, you are a kid. And as a kid, you have only one job: dream the biggest dream you can. And your dad and I will try to help you make that dream come true."

"Even airplane school?"

"Yes, even airplane school."

"Okay, I guess . . ." I reply.

She looks at my lips. "Oh no, are you pouting?" she says with a smile.

"No, no, I'm not pouting!"

"It's too late, I saw you pouting. You know what that means . . . spider fingers!"

She wiggles her fingers and starts tickling me. I squirm and wiggle uncontrollably as I laugh. She tickles me again and again. Everyone in the village can hear my laugh because it's a super laugh. The kind you can't stop even when you try really hard.

"Okay, okay. I'm not pouting anymore, Mom."

She stops tickling me and hugs me extra tight. When the hug is over, there are tears in her eyes.

"What's wrong, Mom?"

She blinks them away quickly. "Ba-Ba, your dad and I . . . we love you."

"Mom, I already know that. The sky is changing colors. It's all gray. The rain is coming. Can I go play now, please?"

She laughs softly, shakes her head, and says, "Go get your bathing suit and the soap."

I zip back to our house, quickly put on my bright yellow bathing suit, and rub soap all over myself. I run out to the front porch. The air is cold, and thunder rumbles in the sky.

It's coming . . . it's coming . . . BOOM! The sky opens up, and it starts to rain. It's raining so hard, it's like the sky is arguing with the earth.

"It's here! It's here!" I yell.

There are kids already playing in the rain. Darn it, I'm late! Stephanie is in her red bathing suit, calling for me to come and get wet with her. A few houses away, Paul signals he wants to race. I'm ready! I run off the porch, but Mom stops me because I forgot to rub soap behind my ears and behind my neck.

"Aw, Mom!" I say as she rubs the soap behind my ears. When she's done, I run out to the center of the village with my friends and shout, "Here's the rain! Here's the rain!" And we take off running. We zoom through the village with our hands held up high in the air. We open our mouths wide and swallow plump drops of rain. We race. We dance. We laugh.

When our parents finally drag us back inside, the rain has gone and night is falling. I get ready for bed, but not really, because tonight is the first of the month. And every first of the month, the grownups gather in the center of the village and tell ghost stories. This time they are telling stories on the front porch of Madame Tita's house because the center of the village is still full of muddy water.

I love, love, *love* story time. I'm not talking about bedtime stories with happy endings. I'm talking about grown-up story time with real-life tales of ghosts and creatures of darkness.

We aren't allowed to listen to the stories. The grownups always send us to bed. But *going* to bed and *staying* in bed are two different things. So on story night when my mom says, "Gabrielle, it's bedtime," I do as she says and lie down. But then I get up, and so do all my friends. We sneak into the center of the village and overhear the best and scariest stories ever told.

There are tales of witches who take your smile away for good if you back out of a deal, or warlocks who take your breath in the night if you wrong them.

My favorite stories are always the ones about people going on adventures. They face impossible tasks and deadly foes. Sometimes the people in the story lose an ear in battle or leave behind a finger or even an eyeball. It's gross and creepy; in other words, it's awesome!

When I take in the stories, I get so caught up in the adventure that I sometimes forget to blink or breathe. Stephanie has to poke me in the ribs, and only then do I let the air back into my lungs. She saves my life once a month.

I think story time should be all the time. But as soon as the sun comes up, it's back to chores. My friends and I have to help out our families by fetching water from the well, which is really far away. We have to sweep and mop the floors. We walk to the market and sometimes carry baskets of food on our heads under the blazing-hot sun. Going to the market is hard, but not going at all is worse. That means your family doesn't have enough money for food.

Some of my friends' families are split apart because the parents can't afford to keep any more kids. So they send some of their kids off to live with relatives in other villages. Some of the people I know don't own shoes and have to ask a neighbor for something to wear on their feet. The people in my village come together, and we help each other with food and clothing.

Also, we don't always have electricity. We have to use gas lamps or candlelight. The meat at the market is expensive, and often we have to go without it. And lately, even the rice has gotten costly. Sometimes we eat cornmeal porridge instead, because a handful of it makes a pot big enough to feed two families.

Most of the grownups in the village are merchants, including my parents. It's hard because the road they have to take to the market is unpaved, rocky, and often full of mud. It takes them forever to get to the market and forever to get back home.

The absolute worst part of my homeland is violence. It comes from a group of soldiers with unlimited power called Macoute. They are tall and thin, like pencils. They wear tan, ugly uniforms and even more hideous hats. They enter villages and trample over everything. They take people away, and their families never see them again. And if you try to resist, the Macoute will hurt you.

They came one night for Stephanie's brother, Jean-Paul. We tried to hide him and help him get away, but they found him. They hit him over and over until he didn't move anymore. We had a funeral, and everyone cried. Stephanie's mom, Mrs. Almé, cried the hardest and the longest.

Ever since then, every night I walk by Mrs. Almé's bedroom, I see the shadow of a flowing river. It's a river she made with her tears. I call it Night River because it only exists at night. Tonight, I see the Night River, but this time, Mrs. Almé is drowning in it. I can smell the salt in the water and feel the heaviness of her body as it begins to sink to the bottom. I rush inside her house.

I was right. The Night River overflowed and threatened to carry her away for good. Everyone in the village comes to see what is happening. But all they see is Mrs. Almé with her eyes closed, twisting and twitching out of control. They can't see the river.

"Madame Tita, I know what's wrong!" I shout.

"Then help her, Gabrielle!"

Suddenly, I'm standing on a bluff. Below me is the raging, wrathful river. The wind howls in my ears and the cold air whips through my nightgown. It makes my whole body tremble. Mrs. Almé's body is being picked up and thrown around by the current. She's going under!

Not if I can help it!

"Night River, you can't have her!" I shout as I leap off the bluff and down into the abyss.

The river fights me, but I stay strong. I wrestle and punch at the waves. I dive deeper and deeper down into the freezing river. I see Stephanie's mom. She is about to sink into the floor of the river. I swim down to her and latch onto her nightgown. Together we head toward the surface. Suddenly, something with tentacles grabs hold of her ankle and wraps around it.

I know what the creature is—an octopus. But not just any kind of octopus. This one feeds on loss and loneliness. But I won't let it get her. I hold her face in my hands and concentrate. I focus on the one thing that could fight off the creature —memory.

I place all the memories of Stephanie and her family in my eyes. Mrs. Almé sees the images reflecting in my eyes like a moving photo album. She starts to remember all the people who love her. She kicks the creature in the face—hard. It lets go, and together we burst through the surface of the water.

In a flash, the river dries up, and we are back in Mrs. Almé's bedroom, breathless and soaking wet. She pulls her daughter close and hugs her for a long time.

Later, I ask my mom why I was the only one who saw the river. She says I'm sensitive and have a gift—I'm able to see what others typically don't.

The next day, I wake up with a feeling in my bones, just like Madame Tita. But this isn't a feeling about the weather. It's a feeling of change. Something huge is about to happen.

After my parents tell me the news, I realize I was wrong. It wasn't a huge change, it was a gigantic change—we are heading to America!

America is heaven. I've never been there before, but all of us kids have heard the rumors. We know that in America, everyone gets electricity, twenty-four hours a day. Also, there are jobs in America, and not just selling stuff in the markets. I heard the country has so much money that the streets are paved with gold coins! That's right, free money on the street. And no one picks it up because they all have enough money and don't need more.

Also, the best part about America—free school!

Parents don't have to pay for their kids to go to school. That means I won't have to stay home if my parents don't have enough money to send me to class. It means that I can go to school full-time!

And food is everywhere. I heard of this thing where you

go to a restaurant, and the staff just keeps bringing you more and more food. They never stop! It's called a "buffet." Can you believe it? The food never ever stops!

When anyone gets a chance to go to America, the village celebrates, because whoever goes to America sends back money to help the villagers they left behind. So if one family goes, it helps the other twelve families back home. I am so excited, Stephanie and I jump up and run around the village, and it isn't even raining. But then we get some not-so-good news: my parents could not get the papers they needed, and so I will have to move to America alone!

"It's okay, Ba-Ba," my mom says. "You will stay with Uncle John and his family. And we will come as soon as we can."

"But I don't want to go without you," I say.

My dad picks me up and places me on his lap. "Ba-Ba, you will have to be brave. Many families do not travel together when they first go to America. You will need to be strong because it's what the family needs from you. You can do this. We know you can," he says as he kisses my forehead.

"Daddy, I don't know Uncle John very much. What if he doesn't like me? What if my aunt doesn't like me? Or their kids don't like me? What if—"

My mom takes my hand in hers and says, "Ba-Ba, no matter what, you have to promise us this—you will not give them any trouble. You cannot misbehave and get sent back here. It would break our hearts. Do you understand?"

I know what she means. Every once in a while, a kid goes

to America and gets sent back to Haiti for misbehaving. They call those kids *timoun pa bon*. That means "no-good kid." No one wants to be sent back, because when you get sent back, the village people are cold and mean to you because you wasted a chance many of them will never get.

"Promise us. Promise that you will not be sent back for bad behavior," Dad says as he looks earnestly into my eyes.

"Yes, I promise. I will behave, and I won't get sent back."

When I think about going to America without my parents, my stomach feels like it's slipped down to my toes and my heart is running away from my body. But I will be strong for my family. And in the end, I'm happy I made the promise to behave myself. It will be an easy promise to keep; after all, I'm going to heaven. How hard can it be to be happy in heaven?

CHAPTER TWO
Lady Lydia

WHEN THE VILLAGE FOUND OUT that I was going to America, everyone worked together to make sure I was "respectable" looking. I wasn't sure what that really meant. But from what I can tell, being respectable means cutting my playtime in half. For the next few days, I was shuttled from one appointment to the next. It was awful.

I had to go see Mrs. Farah, the seamstress, so she could measure me for a new dress. Then I had to go to the street market to find shoes, which took a long time because my mom and the shoe salesman couldn't agree on a price. I told him that he should just lower his price because my mom was really good at haggling, but he didn't listen. And in the end, Mom paid exactly what she wanted to pay and not a penny more. I guess that's her gift.

I spend most of the day with my mom, getting things ready for my trip. I thought I would get to play later, but it's later and I'm standing on Mrs. Farah's porch getting poked by her sewing needles as she measures me again. I can hear the other kids playing now that their chores are done. I want to be out there with them, but I guess I can't.

"Stay here. I need more safety pins," Mrs. Farah says as she disappears into the house.

"Why are you wearing that face?" my dad asks as he comes up the steps and onto the porch. I shrug and look away. "I see —no time to hang out with your friends, huh?"

"No . . ." I grumble.

He peeks inside and then whispers in my ear, "Well, you've been a really good girl. I think the measuring can wait for a few hours."

"Really, Dad?"

"Go ahead. Don't tell your mom," he says.

"Yes!" I shout as I leap up and hug him.

We hear Mrs. Farah's footsteps coming toward us. "Go!" Dad whispers. I take off as fast as I can and join my friends.

Later that night, Stephanie gives me a gift—her favorite seashell. It's pink with gold edges and can fit inside the palm of my hand.

"Are you sure you want to give this away, Stephanie?"

"Yes, that's what best friends do. I want you to have it."

"Thank you." I smile.

She starts to cry. "What's wrong?" I ask her.

"You're going to forget me. Everyone that goes to America forgets friends back home."

"That's not true. People from our village who go to America always send back money and gifts."

"Yeah, but they can't send back time. You and I won't have time together anymore."

"Oh, that's true. How about this: You take my bracelet, the one my mom got me at the market. When you hold it, it's like you're spending time with me. And I will hold your seashell and spend time with you. So we won't ever really be without each other," I tell her as I take off my beaded bracelet and hand it to her. She takes it from me, and we hug for the last time.

When I get home, my mom makes a small hole in the shell and puts it on a chain for me. Then I start getting ready for bed, and she begins to hum. It's her favorite song—a Haitian song about love and family.

She always hums it, and she doesn't even realize she's doing it. I tell her that it makes me sad that I won't hear her hum her song. She promises to call me and sing it if I get lonely. It's not the same, but I nod and say, "Okay." After all, I promised to be brave.

———

Saying goodbye to Stephanie and all my friends and family was hard—but I didn't cry. Well, I did, but I wiped the tears away quickly before they ran down my face, so that doesn't count. Before my dad let me go, he hugged me extra, extra tight. And Mom cried. I made her promise not to cry while I was away, and Dad said he'd make sure she laughed more than she cried. And just before I got on the plane, my mom whispered to me, "You are never alone. You carry our love with you. Always."

When I step onto the plane, all I want to do is run up and down the aisles. I've pictured what the inside of a plane would look like, but this is even better. It has more room than I thought. A lady in uniform shows me to my seat.

I ask her questions—a lot of them. She speaks Haitian Creole, so she understands me and answers. She also gives me extra peanuts and soda. Best trip ever.

It takes a long time to reach America, so long that I actually fall asleep. When I wake up, we are about to land. I look out the window at all the lights below. *Hello, America, I'm here!*

I step out of the plane and into the airport. It's a giant, endless room with bright lights and colorful plastic chairs. I've never seen this many people gathered in one place. They walk by me with their passports and luggage. They move quickly and don't even stop to look at all the wonders around them.

I don't understand how they could keep walking and not touch everything. I want to touch as many things as I can: the staircases that move all by themselves, the large American flag that's as big as a house, and the shops with candy and magazines.

I'm surrounded by the best smells: coffee from the shop on my left and sweet perfume from the shop on my right.

And all around me, people are speaking different languages. I know they are real languages, but they sound funny and made-up. I'd like to walk over and say hello, but my heart starts to beat really fast, and my stomach starts to do somersaults.

What if I'm waiting at the wrong spot? What if Uncle John forgets to pick me up and I have to stay here? I won't be able to tell anyone who I am or where I'm from because my English isn't very good.

Just when I think I'm going to stay here forever, I hear someone call out my name.

"Gabrielle!"

I turn my head and see Uncle John in the crowd waiting for me. Uncle John looks like he's gained three hundred pounds! How'd he get so big?

"Uncle John?" I ask.

He laughs and hugs me. "I know, Gabrielle, I'm a plump apple."

Actually, he looks more like a watermelon. But I think that might be rude to say, so I stay quiet.

"It's the weather. New York City gets really cold in February. We have to dress in many layers to stay warm," he explains as he takes my suitcase. He tells me to follow him. We walk toward the double glass doors, and they slide open.

How do they know when it's time to part and when it's time to close?

I want to ask my uncle, but there's no time for that, because as soon as the doors slide open, an icy gust of wind picks me up and blows me off my feet.

"Gabrielle, hold on!" Uncle John says.

I reach for the door. I'm hanging off the side. My teeth are cubes of ice. My lips are frozen in a smile, and my eyeballs are about to glaze over with frost. My fingers slip, and I am forced to let go of the only thing that's keeping me in America.

Oh no!

Thankfully, my uncle grabs me just as I'm about to get blown back to Haiti. He holds me in place until the sliding doors close again.

He laughs at me and says, "Welcome to America, Gabrielle!"

When we finally get into my uncle's car, my teeth are still chattering. And I feel pain in places I've never felt pain before.

"Your ears are red, and so is your nose. We are going to have to get you a big, warm coat, or you won't last this winter," he says.

"Th-th-thank you," I reply, unable to feel my lips.

Uncle John fiddles around with some of the buttons in his car, and suddenly a stream of warm air fills the car. I start to defrost. Thank goodness.

"I've never been this cold—ever!" I tell him.

"You'll get used to it. Don't worry," Uncle John promises.

I remind myself that it doesn't matter how cold it gets—I am going to stay and behave. I can't believe I made it here. I'm actually in America! I look out the window in amazement. There are streetlights turned on everywhere. I've never seen streets with so many lights before. There isn't one patch of darkness anywhere. The city is alive!

As my uncle drives, I see things I never thought I'd see in real life: paved roads that run smooth and don't have a ditch in the middle. There are shiny, fancy cars on either side of me, and all around me are impossibly tall buildings. It looks like a kingdom of glass and light. I don't see any coins on the ground—maybe everyone got to them first. That's okay; this is heaven, and I am happy to be here.

When we get out of the car, I brace myself for the cold. Now that I know what it's like, I can handle it better. My uncle opens the car doors, and once again the frozen breath of America shouts into my face.

I was wrong; I'm not better at handling the cold. My face feels like someone is pricking it with a needle. I'm so cold that my bones are frozen over. If someone pushed me down right now, I would crack in a hundred pieces. Uncle John shields me from the wind as much as he can as he walks us over to the entrance of a faded tan building that stretches halfway down the block. It looks like it could touch the sky. We enter the large hallway, and I feel like I'm standing in a palace.

"How many people live here?" I ask. My voice echoes back to me.

"Many, many families."

"What's this place called?"

"This place doesn't have a name, only a street number. But this area is called Brooklyn," he says.

"Wow, that sounds magical."

He laughs. "It's an interesting place, all right. Come, let's go inside."

We walk up a flight of stairs and enter Uncle John's apartment. It's smaller than I thought it would be but it's still pretty nice.

"Everyone, come and meet Gabrielle," Uncle announces.

Aunt Carole is the first to greet me. I have never met her before; I've only seen pictures of her. She is tall and chunky, with a nice smile. She has big glasses that take up most of her face. Her skin is the color of my palm.

"Hello," I say with a smile.

"Hello, young lady. We are happy to have you," she says.

"Thank you."

"There is only one rule here: don't get into trouble. Is that clear?" Aunt Carole says.

"Ah, yes. Okay," I reply. I'm not really sure what kind of trouble she's talking about, but I agree, because whatever trouble comes my way, I will avoid it. That's part of the vow I made to Mom and Dad.

I hear the sound of tiny feet stomping toward us. It's my twin cousins, James and Jack. They are two years old, and they look exactly alike. They enter the room holding a big red ball that's way too big for them.

"Play!" one of them says to me.

"I'm sorry, I don't know which is which," I admit.

"The one with the birthmark on his forehead is James. And the one without is Jack," Uncle John says.

"Hi, James!" I call out.

"Play!" he replies. His brother joins in.

"Sorry, boys. It's too late for playtime. And Gabrielle needs to unpack," Uncle John says.

"I'll play with you later, okay?" I tell them. Their eyes light up, and they run over to their mother.

"Kayla, come say hello to your cousin," my aunt calls out.

Kayla enters the room. She has on jeans and a sweater with someone's face on it. I can't make out who it is, but I think I saw the same picture in one of the shops in the airport. She's wearing makeup and has really big hair.

"Hey," she says.

"Um . . . hello," I reply.

I start to talk and she quickly stops me. "Just stay out of my way, and I will stay out of yours." And then she heads back down the hallway.

"She's really nice—but she's also a teenager," Uncle John says.

"Come, I will show you where you will be sleeping," Aunt Carole says as she takes my hand. My room is more like a closet. But it does have a window seat, and I think that's just the best thing ever. I have a perfect view of all the people coming and going in the building.

I unpack my stuff and look around the room. Everything in here feels new. And everything outside my window feels extra new.

I sit down on the bed and feel a pain in my heart. I think it's because even though I like the new stuff, I miss the old stuff. I miss the sounds I used to hear outside my window, like traveling merchants calling out to the villagers to let us know what they were selling that day.

My favorite traveling merchant sold fruit. He'd call out to us in a voice so deep and wide that it reminded me of the ocean. We'd hear him and race to the front of the village to buy Spanish limes, pineapples, and bananas. But now I'm in America and the ocean doesn't talk. The new sound coming from my window is the sound of car horns. And that reminds me of . . . car horns.

In Haiti when I open my window at night, I smell a warm breeze and flowers. Maybe this new place will have the same kind of flowers. I turn toward the window and open it—just a little. I take a deep breath and inhale a new scent. I don't smell flowers or warmth. I smell cold. I start to cough and quickly close the window.

I open the door to my room and walk down the short hallway. I need to find something that feels like the old stuff I'm used to. Then I will feel better and maybe I won't miss home so much. I go into the kitchen, hoping to find something familiar.

On the shelves in the kitchen I see food in boxes—a lot of boxes. I see a box with a picture of rice on it. They have rice in a box! I look around some more, and it looks like everything in America comes in a box. I like that. But it still doesn't help me. I need to find something old, something that I'm used to seeing back home.

I'm just about to give up when something on the shelves catches my eye—it's something that every Haitian has in their home. It's something every kid I know hates and all the moms love—*lwil maskriti.*

I stand on the tips of my toes and get the bottle down from the shelf. The label says "castor oil." I guess that's what they call it in America. I open it and smell it. Yup, it's exactly what my mom uses—I know because it smells awful. It smells like a sweaty sock swallowed bad cheese.

In Haiti, if I had a cold, my mom would take out a bowl and fill it with castor oil. Then she'd pour alcohol on top, strike a match, and set it on fire. It was cool to see the small flames spread across the bowl, like fire dancing across a black, shiny pond. She does that to warm up the oil before she puts it on my chest. But once the flames died down, all the fun was over.

My mom would go back and forth across my chest. It felt like I was the dough and my mom was the rolling pin. She'd put the oil all over my body. She'd even put it on my bare feet. When she was finally done, I felt like I was vibrating on the inside.

But the next morning, when I woke up, I'd always feel better. So I guess that's good, but that doesn't mean I like castor oil. If there were one thing I wish I could shoot out into space, it would be castor oil. That was before, but right now, castor oil is my favorite thing; it's the only thing that isn't new.

I go back to my room and try to remember that there is something in the place that I'm used to. And that everything isn't new and strange. A while later, my aunt calls me to the dinner table; everyone is already seated.

I look down at my plate: there's a stick of meat on a long piece of bread, and there's some red goop on top.

"That's a hot dog. You're in America now, and you should start getting used to American food," Uncle John says.

I poke the meat log with my finger. I turn my nose up at it as my finger digs into the soft pink meat.

"Don't play with your food," Uncle John says.

"We made you hot dogs and fries; it's a real American meal. Would you like something else, Gabrielle?" my aunt asks.

"No, the family is having hot dogs, and that's what she'll eat. It's better this way. She needs to get used to American food. No more rice and beans."

"But John—"

"No, Carole. She needs to adjust. And the more time she spends doing everything the way the Americans do, the better for her."

Aunt Carole looks at me with a sad smile. "Give it a try, honey," she says.

"Yeah, try it," Kayla says with a big, fat smirk.

The meat log hasn't gotten better looking since I last dug into it. But it's rude not to eat what you are given, so I take a bite of something called a hot dog. It's cold, salty, and tastes like rubber. I twist my face away from the food, and Kayla laughs.

"You better get used to it," she says.

That's when I start to think about mangoes and all the yummy foods I left behind. My heart hurts. And soon my stomach begins to dance. I have a funny feeling inside.

"You better eat all of it," Kayla tells me.

"It's okay if you need time to finish," Aunt Carole replies.

Kayla shakes her head. "You can't even eat one hot dog —how are you going to make it here?"

"Do they only have hot dogs in America?" I ask.

"No, but the other stuff will be hard to swallow too. So you better start with the hot dog. Unless you can't. In that case, you might as well go back home now."

"Kayla!" Uncle John scolds her.

"I'm just kidding, Daddy," she says. But she's not kidding. I can see it in her eyes—she's daring me to finish my dinner. Well, I can and I will. I shove the whole thing in my mouth at once. Bad idea. I throw up everything—even the peanuts from the plane.

My aunt has to clean up after me, and I feel really bad about it. I was supposed to stay out of the way, and the first thing I do is give her more work to do. I offer to help, but she says it's okay and that I can go take a shower.

I stand under the warm water, and I marvel at how powerfully it flows. It's as hard as the rain. I close my eyes and pretend I'm back home, playing in the rain. But when I open my eyes, it all goes away. No more racing around in the rain with Stephanie trying to keep up with the boys; no more rain dancing or laughing. I step out of the shower and dry off with the towel my aunt left me. I go to my room and put on the pajamas she brought me.

"Do they fit okay?" Aunt Carole asks as she peeks into my room.

"Yes, it's fine. Thank you." I look down. My pink pajamas have teddy bears and trains on them. It's not my favorite, but it feels nice and warm on my skin.

"Gabrielle, come. Sit beside me on the bed," she says. I do as she asks. "Do you know how many jobs your uncle has?"

"Ah . . . one?"

"Nope."

"Um, two?"

"No. He has three jobs!"

"Really? How does he do them all?"

"He works very hard. He works driving a taxi, he works for a company that cleans the parks, and he washes dishes at a restaurant downtown."

"That's a lot of work."

"Yes, it is. And I too have three jobs. I work at a factory making belts, I look after an elderly woman, and I take care of you kids. We don't have a lot of time or a lot of money. So, when we give you something, treat it with care, because we don't have money to replace it. And that goes for your new pajamas. Is that clear?"

"Yes, Auntie."

"Good girl," she says. My uncle knocks on my door, and I tell him he can come in.

"Someone wants to speak to you," he says, handing me the phone.

"Hello?"

"Hello, Ba-Ba, how are you doing?"

"Mom!" I shout loudly.

Kayla marches down the hall and enters my room. "Can I get some quiet, please? I'm trying to sleep."

"Oh, sorry," I reply. "Mom, I miss you!" I whisper into the phone.

"Your dad and I miss you too. We will be there as soon

as we can, but for now, remember, we love you. And we are counting on you." Hearing my mom and dad's voices reminds me just how far away they really are.

"Mom! Did you make the fried pork and plantains I like today? What story are you going to tell the village next month? Is it the one about the ghost in the well? I love that one!"

"Honey, listen. You can't think about back home. Thinking about back home will only make you lonelier. You have to find new adventures in America. Okay?"

"Okay, Mom."

I'm about to tell her about throwing up, but that would make her worry, so I don't say anything. And my mom is right: I need to stay focused on being here and being here to stay. I don't care how many hot dogs I have to eat.

Hot dogs. Argh!

I get into bed and close my eyes. I should be asleep soon. But I'm not. I try to count the number of streetlights we saw on our way here, but I lose track of them. I sigh and sit up in my bed.

It's so hard to know when to sleep and when to wake up. My body wants to sleep, but there are just so many new things that I want to explore. How is a girl supposed to keep her eyes closed in heaven?

Well, Mom did say she wanted me to have adventures in America now . . .

Okay, I'm going to take a quick walk around the building. I won't get into anything crazy. I will just take a nice, relaxing walk so that sleep might come to me. So that when I get back to this apartment, I will be all ready for bed. I tiptoe as quietly as I can out of the apartment. I look at the clock on my way out—it's exactly midnight.

I walk out of the apartment and go into the lobby of the building. A red door appears in the middle of the lobby. I swear it wasn't there before. There are gold and silver butterflies etched all around the doorframe; they spring to life. I smile as I watch them dance.

They land in the palm of my hand, and I bring them up to my face so I can get a closer look. They are so beautiful. They fly away and gather again in the air. They flutter around the door and motion for me to go inside.

"I can't go in. I promised to be good. I promised my mom and dad." The butterflies are sad. But I walk away. It's the smart thing to do. Then I hear someone humming from behind the door. It's a song I know very well. And a voice I know too.

"Mom?"

I walk back and put my ear to the door. The humming gets louder. I turn the red metal knob and walk inside. It's a dimly lit room with smooth walls and shiny black floors. And standing right in front of me, I'm fairly certain, is a witch.

She's thinner than a needle, her skin is the color of fog, and her dark eyes shine like moonbeams on the surface of water. Her lipstick is redder than red, and so are her long, curved nails. She wears a long cloak made up of crows that have gathered around her.

"Hello, Gabrielle," she says in perfect Haitian Creole. That doesn't surprise me. I was told a long time ago that witches speak every language. I was also told that it's a bad idea to speak to them at all. But I'm not afraid of witches—well, not too afraid, anyway. I swallow hard and tell my heart to stop jumping. I can handle this. I think.

"Gabrielle, it's rude not to return a greeting."

"Hello. I thought I heard my mom, but I was wrong. I will go now."

"Wait, my dear, stay awhile," she says. The crows that make up her cloak scatter and form a chair so that I can sit before her.

Nope, not gonna happen.

"Ah, thank you, but I have to go," I reply. I know better than to turn my back on a witch; any fool can tell you that. So I walk backwards to the door. I turn the knob, but it doesn't move.

"I only wanted to welcome you to the neighborhood. My name is Lady Lydia."

"You're a witch," I tell her.

"Well, yes, dear, we both know that. Here, have some juice," she says as a table appears out of nowhere with a pitcher of juice, cups, and wooden chairs.

Whoa!

"No thank you," I reply, trying to sound normal.

"I insist you at least sit while I drink, then," she says. I take a seat, not wanting to upset her. In the meantime, I try to think of possible ways to escape.

"As I said before, I'm Lady Lydia. I'm the witch of these

parts, and I enjoy helping nice, innocent children like you, who just came to this country. I have treats that can really help newcomers like you. In fact, newcomers are my biggest clients." She sips her juice.

"I don't need anything, thank you. I would just like to go home," I reply.

"Well, certainly." She loses her grip on her cup. The juice falls and lands on me.

I quickly jump up. "Oh no!" I shout. "I promised my aunt that I would take care of the things she gave me. My shirt is ruined!" I groan as I look down at my pajamas.

"Oh, is that all?" She waves her hand, and the stain is gone.

Wow. I always knew there were witches, but I've never seen one at work before.

"Um . . . thank you. Thanks very much," I mumble.

"My pleasure. That one was a freebie. I have all kinds of treats that can help you in your time of need. Some of my treats are more expensive than others. But they are all very good and very reliable."

"Yes, I'm sure they are. But I want to go home. That's all I want. And you will open the door. Now," I demand.

She smiles. "I like your brave spirit. I can see why you are so loved. But that's only in Haiti, dear. You are in America now. And here, they won't like you; they won't love you. In fact, you'll stand out and be ridiculed. And that's when you will come to me like the other kids before you. And you'll beg me for one thing."

"One thing? What is that? What will I beg you for?"

"An elixir to make everyone like and accept you."

"No, I won't need one. Open this door," I shout. "Open this door now!" I scream as loud as I can. Suddenly, the door opens wide. I run away as fast as I can.

I hear her footsteps clacking behind me. "You'll be back! They always come back . . ."

CHAPTER THREE
If Only

I WAS GOING TO TELL MY FAMILY about the witch the next day, but I had to go get my hair braided. My aunt let me choose the kind of braids I want. I picked box braids because they are so pretty. But the problem is, they take forever. When I am finally done at the hair place, I'm too tired to talk about the witch. So, I go right to bed.

The day after that, my uncle takes me to get a new coat. I tell him I won't need it because the calendar on the wall in the kitchen says that we are at the end of winter; the month of February will be over in a week.

"I looked it up, Uncle, it's almost March, that means here comes spring. It's going to be warmer."

He laughs and says, "Just because the calendar says winter is coming to an end doesn't mean it won't be cold or that it won't snow. That's how New York City works. The trains are late. And so are the seasons." So we spend the day shopping for a winter coat. He buys me one that's big and thick. It's white and has a hood in the back of it. I look like a cloud with braids. I wanted something smaller and prettier, but my uncle said that winter is not the time to think about fashion.

I should have told them about the witch then, but I was too busy admiring how my new stuff looked on me to worry about a silly witch. By the time I finally remember to tell them, a whole week has already passed. So I decide not to say anything because I don't plan on seeing her again, so it doesn't really matter.

Also, I don't have time to worry about Lady Lydia. My aunt and uncle tell me that my first day of school will be Monday, March fourth. I write it down on the calendar in the kitchen. It's only a few days away, but I feel like it's a hundred years. I try hard not to count the days because they make me too excited.

The weekend before school starts, my aunt takes me shopping for school supplies. We buy so many things! We get rulers, markers, and three different kinds of folders. I wish Stephanie could be here. She'd never believe how many things we get to buy. Thank goodness my aunt said we could get a few small things to send to her. Her favorite color is blue, so I get her a set of blue pencils, a blue folder, and a notebook.

My aunt told me to watch TV so that I can pick up some English. I've been watching, and it's fun, but sometimes they speak way too fast for me. My uncle got me a tape to help me with English, but sometimes listening to it is really boring.

I wish I could just wake up and suddenly know how to speak English really well. But everyone, including my parents, tells me that it will take time. That doesn't seem fair. The weekend is almost over, and so far all I know how to really say is "Hello, my name is Gabrielle. How are you doing? I am good." Is that enough to help me make friends?

It's Sunday night, the night before school, and I can't eat anything because I'm so nervous about my first day. I knock on Kayla's door and ask if she will let me in. I hear her sigh like I just asked for the last slice of pizza.

"Fine. Come in," she says.

I enter her room. It's bigger than mine and has a lot of posters on the wall. I don't know who LL Cool J is, but she must really love him, because his poster hangs over her bed and is twice my size. There's also a guy sitting on a motorcycle wearing a purple suit and more hair gel than Kayla.

I'm so busy looking at all the posters on the wall that I almost forget why I came.

"Gabrielle! What do you want? I'm busy," she says as she adds another layer of eye shadow.

"Is your dad going to let you leave the apartment like that?" I ask.

"What's wrong with it? I look good."

"Okay." I shrug.

"I'm not going out like this. I'm just trying it out. My friends are having a sleepover, and we're doing each other's makeup. I don't want to mess up my friends' makeup, so I'm practicing."

"Can I ask you something?" I say as I wander over to her dresser. I pick up a metal comb with a cord at the end of it.

I've seen these in Haiti, but not with the cord attached. "What is this?"

"You came in here to ask about my straightening comb?"

"Ah, no."

She snatches it out of my hand. "Then ask your question and go. You know I don't like people touching my stuff."

"Yeah, okay. Sorry. I'm going to school tomorrow—my first day. I wanted to know what your first day of school was like when you came to America. Was it good? Was it bad? Did they like you? Do you think they'll like me?" I don't stop to take in air; that's how fast I throw out the questions.

She rolls her eyes and goes back to her makeup. I guess that means she's not gonna help me. I look down at the floor and feel my stomach ache. I'm alone in this.

"Sorry to bother you," I say as I head out the door.

"Gabrielle, wait!"

I turn back to face her. "Yeah?"

"Whatever you are thinking of wearing, don't. It's wrong."

"You haven't even seen what I'm gonna wear."

"Doesn't matter. No matter what you wear, they'll make fun of it."

"Oh."

She sighs and says, "Listen, no matter how bad it is, you only have to do your first day once. And if you get past it, the other days will get better."

I nod sadly. I'd give anything, anything at all, to have Stephanie here with me.

"All right, you don't have to look so sad. You can hang out with me for a little while."

"Really?"

"Yeah. Have you ever heard 'How Will I Know'?"

I shake my head.

"I have so much to teach you." Then she goes over to her stereo and plays a song that makes me move and act crazy —just like back home.

———

The next morning, when my aunt comes into my room to wake me up, she's surprised to find that I have already showered, dressed, and eaten breakfast. I'm sitting on the edge of the bed with my backpack next to me. I'm ready to go—the only trouble is I can't get my legs to work.

"Wow, I see someone is excited for their first day of school," my aunt says.

I look up at her, worried. She smiles and says, "Every-one gets nervous on the first day. Don't worry; you'll make friends."

That's not what Lady Lydia says . . .

"Gabrielle, get up!" my aunt says.

My legs do as they're told. I get up from the bed, take my backpack, and head out of the apartment. My aunt walks me down the block and across the street to where the other kids are waiting for the school bus. There are about twenty kids, all of them speaking really fast. I can't catch most of what they are saying. I hold my aunt's hand even tighter.

"I don't like this, Auntie."

"It will be just fine. Remember how you didn't like hot dogs when you tried them at first?" she says.

"I still don't like them," I tell her.

"Yes, but you tried other things, and you found some things you do like. You like pizza, Cheetos, and apple pie. This is the same thing. You have to give things a try. Now, I have to get ready for work. So, you go stand in the line and wait for the bus, okay?"

I nod, but I don't talk because my mouth is too dry to form words. I watch as my aunt walks away. I miss home. I miss Haiti. I miss my parents and Stephanie. I would give anything to be back there right now.

Okay, Gabrielle, stop that! Try to make friends. You can do it!

I look around the crowds of kids and make myself walk up to one of the girls in line. She has pretty, long hair that hangs high above her head in a ponytail. She's talking to a group of girls. I wait for them to finish before I start to speak. Okay, I can do this.

"Hello, my name is Gabrielle. How good you?"

Everyone at the bus stop laughs at me. Oh no! I think I missed a word. I try again. "Good you how?" They all laugh even harder. My stomach hurts. My fingers are numb, and not just from the cold. But I am not a coward. I try it again. "You good how?" I guess that's wrong too, because the kids all laugh even louder.

They look at me and point. The bus comes and opens its doors so the kids can get on. The kids shove past me and enter the bus. I'm the last one to get on. I walk down the aisle and try to find a place to sit. But as soon as I walk by, students seated next to an open seat place their hands there so that I don't sit down.

My heart sinks down to my toes. No one wants me next to them. They are whispering and giggling about me as I get closer. When I get to the end of the aisle, there is nowhere to sit at all. The bus driver, a big woman with a deep voice, yells at me. "Find a place, young lady. I can't move until you sit down."

I look over at the last seat and the girl who is seated there. She has short, shiny hair and glasses. She folds her arms in front of her and pouts as I move in to sit next to her. Is she going to push me to the floor? No, she doesn't. But everyone knows she's not happy with me being next to her. She keeps her eyes straight ahead and continues to pout.

My chest feels really tight. It's like I have a snake wrapped around me, squeezing me. It hurts. I want to cry and run away. But there's no way to get off the bus. And even if I could, I'd get in trouble for not going to school.

Maybe I don't need school. Maybe I can run away and do something fun that also makes me a lot of money. That way, I can still send money back home. Yes! I will learn to fly planes and do tricks with them. People will pay me, and then I won't need to be on this stupid bus where everyone is mean. But before I can make my escape, we arrive at school.

Once I'm off the bus, I follow the kids into the huge building. It's twice the size of Haiti. There are so many kids, all of them speaking a thousand words every minute. I walk inside and watch as they whiz past me. The teachers hurry us along. But I don't know where to go or what to do.

"You must be the new student, Gabrielle Jean . . . I was looking for you. I'm here to show you to your class," someone says behind me. I turn around and see a tall woman with an Afro and pretty dangling earrings.

"I'm Mrs. Bartell. I'm the librarian here."

"I am Gabrielle," I reply.

"Your file says you are from Haiti. Is that true?" I nod but don't speak. She smiles at me and says, "I am from Haiti too." And then she begins to speak in Haitian Creole to me. I'm relieved. She tells me that there are a lot of families in Brooklyn that came from the Caribbean. There are kids whose families are from Jamaica, Trinidad, and the Dominican Republic.

"They don't talk to me," I say. "I said the wrong thing, and now they hate me."

"No, they don't. Give them a chance to get to know you. You'll make friends; just keep trying. And if you need anything, you can come see me. I'll be in the library. It's on the third floor," she says as she walks me to my class. I stand there in the long hallway looking into the class of kids who already don't like me.

"Guess what, Gabrielle?" Mrs. Bartell says.

"What?" I ask, trying to swallow my fear away.

"I have a whole room full of books about little girls just like you who had to face their fears, and they won."

"A whole room full of books about girls like me?"

"Yes, that's right. Young women who had to face very hard

41

times, and they found a way to beat the odds and win the battle. And they even ended up helping the world become a better place. They made history."

"They were braver than me, Mrs. Bartell. I can't go in."

"I read your file, Gabrielle. I know the part of Haiti you come from. I have family there too. It's a hard life, and yet you managed to survive. If you can do that, then you can do anything."

"But I had my mom and dad then. And my friends."

"Well, now you have me. And I am telling you—you'll be just fine. In fact, you will do really well here. Just remember, you are just as special and just as amazing as the other kids. And don't let anyone tell you differently."

I nod back at her and place my hand on the doorknob. I open the door and enter the classroom. The teacher tells everyone my name, and they say hello in a whisper. Then my teacher tells me to take my seat. I go over to the corner where my seat is and try not to cause any problems. Maybe if I'm quiet, maybe if I don't make a sound, no one will bother me. Maybe I will somehow be invisible.

I'm not. They all see me and dislike me right away. They pass around a note with my name on it. And when I open it up, it's a picture of a monkey. They make fun of my clothes and my hair. They laugh when they see tears in my eyes. I run out of the class and into the hallway. I look until I find a bathroom. I go inside one of the stalls and cry.

"Hello?" someone says from outside.

I stop crying. I don't want anyone to hear me. The person

says hello again. I come out of the stall to see who's there. Someone just left. I walk out to see who it was, but there's no one in the hallway. I'm about to go back in and wash my face when I hear her humming my mom's song—Lady Lydia.

"What are you doing here?" I ask.

"I came to see how your first day was going. Well, actually, I already saw it in the leaves, dear. Your first day has gotten off to a rather bad start."

"It's going to be fine. I don't need your help. Now go away."

"Okay, if you need me, you know where I am." She laughs as she disappears into thin air. On my way back to class, I walk past a large room with rows of white tables. The smell of hot food fills my nose. It actually smells pretty good. I peek inside, and there are endless trays of food on top of the tables. I watch as people with hairnets throw the trays of food into large black bags.

"What are you doing out of class?" Mrs. Bartell says. Her voice startles me.

I turn around. "Where are they taking the food?" I ask.

"That was from the breakfast rush. Many of the kids don't like eating school food, so a lot of it gets thrown away."

"Thrown away?" I shout.

"Unfortunately, yes."

"Can I take some?" I ask.

"Well, I'm sure if you are hungry, they will let you have a tray."

"No, I mean can I take all the trays and send them home —to Haiti?"

"Gabrielle, that's very nice, but that's not how it works."

"Why not? There's a lot of food, and no one is eating it. So let's send it someplace people will eat it."

"I don't think the food will survive the trip. But it's nice that you want to help."

"But I'm not helping. I'm only making this worse. I don't have any money to send back to Haiti like people are supposed to do when they leave the village, and the kids are teasing me. I ran out of class, so I know I'll get in trouble, and I promised my mom . . . Everything is awful, Mrs. Bartell."

"You can help Haiti by staying in class no matter what the other kids say to you. And you need to keep trying to make a new friend. If you stop trying, you won't ever find one. Now, let's get you back in class. Okay?"

I shrug and mumble, "I guess."

The rest of the day isn't any easier. I have to go to ESL. That means "English as a second language." It's a special class for kids who just came to America and need extra help in English. English is much harder than you think. I can't believe that there are three words that sound exactly the same but mean totally different things. These are the words: *merry*, *marry*, and *Mary*. Yup, I don't get it.

And then my ESL teacher asks me to say the word *bathroom*, and I do—I say *bafroom*. She says that's not the right way to say it. It's not my fault that the *th* sound is so hard to make. And when school is over, I have to get back on that stupid bus again, and again, no one wants to sit next to me.

When I get home, all I want to do is get under my covers

and never come out. Well, if my aunt gets us pizza again, I will come out, but only long enough to take two slices and get back under the covers. But dinner isn't pizza, it's liver and onions. Yuck! I don't want any, but my aunt says I can't leave the table until I eat something. I guess I should just be happy that the school didn't call to tell them about me running out. I sigh and poke the liver with my fork.

A few minutes later, my uncle comes home, and, well, things just get worse. We hear him enter before we see him. He's stomping around so hard that it makes the water glasses on the dinner table shake. He enters and slams the door behind him. He's yelling about work, and how they never give him a chance to advance because English is not his first language. I wonder if he knows the difference between *merry*, *marry*, and *Mary*.

Well, even if he does, now is not the time to ask. It takes him five minutes to take off his coat because he's wearing so many layers. When he finally sits down, he plops down on the chair and sulks.

"Honey, everything will be just fine," my aunt says as she gets up, then kisses him on the cheek. She puts his dinner in front of him, but he just grumbles and pushes the food away.

"You're not the only one who had a bad day. Gabrielle did too. Want to share with us, honey?" Auntie says.

I shake my head. I'm just waiting for dinner to be over so I can crawl into my bed.

"My friend's sister goes to Gabrielle's school, and she told me that everyone at school laughed at her," Kayla says.

"Don't pay them any attention," Auntie replies.

"It's her fault. She talks weird," Kayla says. I glare at her. I have decided I am never going to be a teenager. They are really annoying.

"Everyone has bad days," Auntie says.

"Can I go now, please?" I ask.

"Help the twins with their dinner, Gabrielle," Auntie says. I sigh and go over to the twins, who are making a fort out of their food. The phone rings.

"Leave it!" Uncle says to Auntie as she goes to pick it up.

"It could be important," she replies.

"It's Haiti calling—it's always Haiti calling. They need money. And I understand, but we just don't have any right now. So, don't pick up," he says.

She rolls her eyes and picks up the phone. "Hello?" She's quiet for a moment and then hands the phone to my uncle.

"Who is it?" he asks.

"Haiti," she says.

He groans and takes the call. I help feed the twins and then go to my room. A few minutes later, the phone rings again. I guess Haiti is calling once again. But I'm wrong. It's my school. My aunt and uncle enter my room. "Gabrielle, did you storm out of class today?"

"Ah . . . today . . . kind of," I reply in a small voice.

My uncle begins to yell—very loudly. His eyes grow extra wide in his head. The picture frames in my room shake. The bears printed on my pajamas run for cover and hide behind the printed trains.

"School is not optional, young lady! If I ever hear of you missing class again, I will call your parents. Is that clear?"

"But Uncle, everyone was laughing at me. They didn't want to be friends—"

"No buts, missy! You came here for school, not to make friends. So if no one wants to be your friend, you will have to learn to be your own friend. You are here for an education, not a social life. And you will never walk out of class again. Do you hear me?"

"Yes, sir."

"Now go to bed. You have school in the morning, and so help me, if you are late . . ."

I get into bed, and he closes the door behind him.

I want to go home. I want to be back in Haiti where it's warm, and the people are nice. I want to be home where the aroma of my mom's rice and beans fills the house and makes it smell wonderful. I need to hear Stephanie shouting my name to come play and challenge the boys. I miss home so much I ache.

Someone knocks on my door. It's my aunt. She asks if she can come in, but I don't say anything. It's her house; she'll come in anyway. She enters and comes over to my bed. She gently rubs my back and speaks in a soft voice.

"It's okay, honey. It's all gonna be okay."

"Uncle is mad. He yelled at me," I reply.

"Yes, I know. But he's not really mad at you. He's upset because we have so many mouths to feed back home. It seems like no matter how much money we make, it's impossible to help send things back home and take care of our family here.

"Every time the phone rings, it's some family member from Haiti who needs something. And while they really need it, sometimes we don't have it."

"I thought everyone in America was rich," I say.

"Yes, that's what many people think until they get here. America isn't as hard to live in as Haiti can sometimes be, but it still has its challenges. Being an immigrant, Gabrielle, is hard. That's why your uncle wants you to do your best and focus on learning. You are your parents' only hope at a better future. You have to try your absolute best to make things work at school. Everything depends on it."

I try to put the first day of school out of my head as I fall asleep. I keep telling myself that tomorrow is a brand-new day.

———

I wake up to the sound of my uncle and Kayla in the middle of an argument. Their voices carry out into the hallway and right into my room.

"But why, Daddy?"

"Because I said no."

"It's just a sleepover! Why can't I go? My other friends are going."

"I do not care what other people do. You are my daughter and I will not let you sleep at someone else's house!"

They continue to argue as I go into the bathroom to wash

up. After my shower, I get dressed and fix my hair, and still the two of them are arguing. My aunt comes into my room and tells me to hurry or I won't have a chance to eat before I have to catch the bus.

"Are they still fighting?" I ask.

"Yes. They are worse than the twins."

I finish getting dressed and follow my aunt to the kitchen. My uncle and Kayla are looking at each other the same way I look at Paul from my village before we race against each other.

"What is the big deal? It's what they do here. It's what everyone does in America," Kayla says.

"When you come through that door, you are not in America. You are in Haiti. This apartment is Haiti. And in Haiti, we do not let our kids sleep in a stranger's house."

"That's not fair!" she shouts.

"Hey, watch your tone with your father," my aunt warns as she stuffs the twins into their coats.

"Tell me, what is wrong with your bed?" my uncle asks. "It cost a lot of money, and now you don't want to sleep in it? Why?"

"It's not about the bed. I want to spend time with my friends," Kayla says.

I make my way over to the pot of oatmeal on the stove and serve myself. I want to go before my uncle really loses his temper.

"You go to school with them, you talk to them on the

phone, and you want more time together? What craziness is this? You have a bed here, and here is where you will sleep, every night!" he shouts.

"You don't understand. You are ruining everything!"

"That is my job. I am your father, not your friend."

Now I have my oatmeal, but I need a spoon. The only way to get to the spoons is to get past my uncle and Kayla. Oh no . . .

"If you are going to make this apartment like Haiti, then you should let me sleep over at my friend's house. Mom said sometimes she would do that as a kid in Haiti."

"When we have to sleep in other people's houses, we do not do it for fun. We do it because there's a revolt. When there is a revolt in Brooklyn, you can sleep at your friend's house."

"I hate this place. It's a prison!" Kayla shouts.

He looks her over. "Prison doesn't have hair gel! It cost me four dollars!"

Okay, I don't need a spoon. I put the bowl to my lips and drink as much as I can, then quickly drink the juice on the table. I say goodbye to both my uncle and Kayla. My aunt does the same, then she grabs the twins and we flee the war zone.

When I get to the bus stop, I stand in line and keep my head down. There's a girl standing next to me, a girl I don't remember from yesterday. She seems nice. I try to talk to her.

"Hello, I am Gabrielle. How are you doing?"

Yes! I think I got that right. But judging by her face, she can't understand me. But unlike the other kids, she doesn't laugh; she just looks confused. It's my accent. It's thick and hard to understand. The rest of the day goes by pretty much the same way. Even if I am able to get a smile from one of the kids, my accent gets in the way.

"Argh! If only I could get rid of my accent. Then everyone would like me," I shout to no one as I make my way down the school hallway.

"Funny you say that. I believe I have just the thing . . ."

I follow the voice behind me. It's Lady Lydia! My eyes grow to the size of melons and my jaw drops. I quickly look around the hallway to see if anyone else has spotted her. Thankfully, the hallway is clear. In Haiti, witches aren't bold enough to appear in the daytime. But Lady Lydia is in the school again!

"What are you doing here?" I ask as I check the hallways once again to make sure we are alone.

"Dear, only you can see me—so long as that's what I want," she says.

Phew, no one else can see her. Thank goodness. I look her over. She's wearing the same outfit and has the same shrill laugh. The only different thing is me—this time I don't want to shoo her away. This time, I want to know more . . .

CHAPTER FOUR
Pale

LADY LYDIA STANDS IN FRONT OF ME, waiting for me to tell her to go away. And that's what I should do—that's what a smart girl would do. And I am—I'm very smart. But I'm also a little curious. There's nothing wrong with that, is there?

"Oh my, I'm so sorry to take up your time like this, Gabrielle. You've made it very clear that you are not interested in my help. I will go now. Enjoy the rest of the school day, dear." She starts to walk away.

When her sharp heels hit the shiny surface of the hallway floor, they make a clicking sound. Her steps fall in line with the pounding of my heart. Her walk is slow but steady. And with each click, each heartbeat, I become desperate.

What if her magic is the only way I will ever make friends? What if I'm standing here doing nothing while my only hope for happiness gets away, one click at a time?

"Lady Lydia, wait!"

She stops but doesn't turn around.

"Yes?" she says in a deep, booming voice.

"I was thinking. It's rude not to listen when someone has something to say—even if that someone is a witch."

"Are you saying you're interested in my help?"

"I'm saying . . . maybe," I reply, and swallow hard.

She slowly turns to face me. Her mouth curls into a crooked smile and her eyes gleam with delight. She places her hands together, making her needle-like fingertips collide with each other.

"Come closer, dear," she says.

I take a step toward her, and then another. And another. I'm tingling. Yes, I could be heading for danger, but I could also be heading for a whole new life.

"Now, why don't you tell me what it is you'd like my help with?" she says.

"Um . . . well. I don't know. I mean, I do, but . . ." I know exactly what I want help with, but why can't I just say it out loud?

"Dear, are you embarrassed?"

Yes.

"No, I'm not," I reply, unable to look her in the eye.

"It's okay. Many people have trouble making friends and fitting in. That's why I'm here. To make sure you get everything you want."

"Let's say I did have trouble making friends—and I'm not saying I do. But if I did, what would you be able to do for me?"

"Oh, so many things. I can create something to make all your troubles go away. You'd fit right in with everyone at this school. You'd have friends, you'd be popular, and you'd be liked—loved! You'd be loved by everyone at school, but most importantly, you would belong. Don't you want to belong, Gabrielle?"

"Yes!"

The word jumps out of my throat before I have a chance to stop it. It's a bad idea to let a witch know just how much you want what they have to offer. But it's too late. I can tell by the wild expression in her eyes that she knows she has something that I want—no, something that I need. I need to belong, no matter what. It's pointless; I might as well come out and say it.

"Lady Lydia, I want everyone at school to like me, to be my friend. I want to . . ."

"Say it, Gabrielle."

"I want to belong."

"Lucky for you, I've got just the thing . . ."

"Really? Where is it? Can I have it now?"

She laughs. "Oh no, the school hallway isn't the proper place to finish this conversation. If you want my help, you'll have to meet with me later."

"Where?"

"Midnight. Under the faded red bridge in Prospect Park.

"Midnight at Prospect Park?!"

"Yes, I would imagine it will be difficult to sneak away, but you strike me as a resourceful young lady, Gabrielle. I think you'll figure out a way to get past your aunt and uncle."

My heart sinks. My aunt and uncle have been going to bed later because the twins have had a cough. What if they are still awake by the time I have to go out? Lady Lydia studies me and then says, "Okay, fine. I hate to see a young lady as desperate as you struggle." She whisks her right hand in the air, and a small blue vial appears in the palm of her hand.

"This is called 'Pale,'" she says as she holds out the blue vial. I step back. I'm no fool; I can't just drink whatever a witch gives me, any kid knows that.

"Are you afraid? Don't be. It's perfectly safe," she says.

"How can I be sure?"

"It's a little something I whipped up to help a client of mine; his name was Gus. He wanted to be invisible so that he could sneak past his wife and eat the delicious pies she made in their family bakery. She's only allowed him to have one slice a week. He came to me, and I gave him this. He became invisible and ate as many pies as he wanted."

"What happened to him?" I ask.

"He ate so much he became bigger than the state of New York. He popped wide open. Parts of Gus fell all over the city. It was like human confetti."

She laughs wickedly as she offers it to me. I scrunch my face, disgusted. I back away from the blue bottle.

"Gabrielle, dear, I'm just kidding."

"Gus is fine?"

"Gus is . . . He's exactly where he belongs. Now go ahead and take it."

"This could be a trick. I know your kind, and I won't be tricked into drinking something bad."

She opens the vial and pours a single drop on her left

hand; while her body remains in the hallway, her left hand disappears.

"Like I said, this is to help you get out of your home unseen."

I step closer to the vial and watch as her left hand returns. The vial really does make things disappear and reappear again. "So, I drink this and then disappear?"

"But only for five minutes. Whatever happens, you need to be out of your house in that five minutes, or they will see you."

"So if I don't move fast enough, I'll get caught and be in big trouble?"

"Only you will know if it's worth the risk. The question you have to ask yourself is this: How much do you want to belong?"

———

For the rest of the school day, all I can think about is my meeting with Lady Lydia. I don't hear any of the things my teachers say. When the school day is over, I get on the bus. I have to do my least favorite thing: walk down the aisle of the bus and hope someone lets me sit next to them. But no one wants me to. So I sit alone.

Normally, I would feel really bad, but today, I am okay sitting by myself in the back of the bus. I need time to think. I can't just drink the vial of Pale and make a run for it. I have to plan my exit carefully.

Back in Haiti, there was a merchant who sold ice at the market. We called him the Ice Man. Sometimes we kids would have enough money to buy fresh lemonade from the Lemon Lady, but we didn't have enough money to buy the ice to make the lemonade cold. There's nothing sadder than warm lemonade.

Some of the merchants at the market were really nice, giving us a free taste of their products, but not the Ice Man. He wouldn't even give us a small piece of ice to split among us. In fact, he trained his dog to smell for us kids and to bark if we approached his large white bucket of ice.

So Stephanie and the rest of us kids had to come up with a plan. One of us would start to dance and play music near the Ice Man. He hated noise, and he hated kids. So he'd chase us down, leaving his ice bucket for his dog to guard. The meat merchant was a friend of my mom's, and she'd give us a thick, juicy bone to feed the dog. The dog would be too busy with his snack to notice us creeping up and taking handfuls of ice. We had to know exactly which route to take in order to get away fastest, or the ice would melt. I was the one who came up with the plan. I don't want to brag, but I was always really good at making plans.

This time things will be easier; there's no dog to worry about. I just need to get past my family and not bump into anything. Yes, I will have the vial to help me, but if I smash into something and make a noise, I will be found out. I take out a pen and paper to write out my plan. Someone rips the paper from my hands.

"Hey!" I shout.

I look up to see who it is; her name is Tianna Thompson.

She's taller than a tree, with big owl eyes that seem to spot me wherever I am. And when she finds me, her mouth morphs into a bullhorn so she can amplify her teasing me.

Behind her is a pod of dolphins. Okay, they are really just students like me, but that's what they remind me of. They hunt in a pack, they sway in unison, and they follow whatever Tianna says and does. So now that Tianna has decided to tease me, they all join in.

I should have taken my time to find the right words in English to tell them to give me my stuff back. But I can't think of the right words. And I'm getting more and more upset as Tianna waves the paper just above my head. English is a hard language to learn, but when I'm upset, it gets even harder.

I jump higher and higher to get my paper, and on the last try, I fall to the floor of the bus; Tianna and the dolphins laugh at me. Then she rips the paper right above my head. The pieces rain down on me. My face gets warm and my hands tremble with anger.

One of the kids on the bus, the girl I tried to speak to this morning, extends her hand to me. I want to take it, but what if she's just trying to embarrass me? I shake my head and get up by myself. That's one thing I know: I'm all by myself in this country—at least until I get help from Lady Lydia. She'll solve all of my problems.

———

That night when I'm sure it's all clear, I drink the vial of Pale. My body tingles and gets really warm. It feels like I need to sneeze. Oh no, that might wake someone up! But there's no stopping it. I'm going to sneeze—but instead, I disappear.

That's so cool!

Gabrielle, focus! You only have five minutes.

I leave my room and head down the dark hallway. I have to get past the bathroom, the kitchen, and finally the front door. I mapped this out in my head, so even though it's dark, I know exactly where I am going. I place my hands on the wall and feel my way around, but I hear . . .

"Gabrielle! Don't do that!"

My heart drops to my feet and then melts through the floorboards. It's my cousin, Kayla.

She's sleepwalking!

"Keep away from my stuff. My stuff!" she says, in a deep sleep.

"Okay, Kayla. No one will touch your stuff. C'mon, let's go back to bed." I gently guide her back to her room.

Her voice changes into a high, girly sound. "Oh, Donnie, I love you too," she says as she puckers up to kiss the leader of her favorite rap group. I twist my face in disgust. Gross. I tuck her in, and she starts to snore peacefully. I walk out of Kayla's room and see my uncle sneaking a late-night snack in the kitchen.

I look at my watch. I only have two more minutes to get out of the house. I quickly make my way past the other room. I need to make a run for it.

One minute.

I try to run past the kitchen, but instead, I trip on one of the twins' toy trucks and slide clear across the room. I'm headed right for the kitchen window—the closed window. There's a fly near the wall that's headed for the same window as I am. In half a second, both of us will be smashed to death.

"Open the window!" I shout.

Uncle turns around and sees nothing.

"Who said that?" he asks. He looks over at the fly. "Did you speak, fly? Hmm . . . I thought only flies in Haiti talk. I guess not."

"Open. Now!" I yell.

My uncle opens the window. And both the fly and I hurtle through the opening down onto a small mound of snow. The fly takes off. My uncle calls out from the window, "Be free, fly; be free!" Then he closes the window and backs away, just as I am visible again.

Phew! That was close.

I get up and make my way to the witch.

CHAPTER FIVE
Prospect Park

IT'S SNOWING NOW, and the wind is howling in my ears. I put on a lot of layers so I wouldn't be cold. It doesn't work. I'm chilled to the bone, but I don't think it's because of the weather. I think that any time you are headed to meet a witch, your bones get cold.

"Hey! What's the big idea?" someone says in a high-pitched voice.

I look around but don't see anyone.

"Down here, kid!" someone says.

I look down on the ground and see a large black rat, with his paws folded across his chest, scowling.

"Rat!" I shriek, and take cover behind the bushes.

"Typical human. You ruin my home and then make me look like the bad guy!"

"Are you talking to me?" I ask.

"Do you see anyone else around here, destroying my house?"

"Your house?" I ask from behind the bush. I peek out a little. "All I see is trash."

"That's what I said, my house!"

I look closer at the small pile of trash, and there's a hole. I guess that's the doorway. And he's right. I trampled it.

"Oh, I'm sorry. I didn't see it," I say.

"Well, that doesn't help me at all! You humans, think you can do whatever you want. Get out from behind that bush and put 'em up!" he says and makes two fists. He moves around like a boxer.

I stand up and face him. I am scared of rats, but tonight is not a night for fear. After all, if I'm brave enough to stand up to a witch, a rat should be easy, right?

"I didn't mean to trash your . . . trash."

"No! Rocky's taking a stand! Put 'em up!"

I check the pink plastic watch my aunt gave me. I have a few minutes before I have to meet Lady Lydia.

"It was your house. I messed it up, and I'm sorry. I don't have a lot of time, but I will help you rebuild it, okay?"

"Well, I suppose that's all right. The house wasn't that great. I ate a big chunk of the roof earlier—I was hungry."

I carefully reach into my coat pocket and hand him a candy bar. His eyes light up. He gladly takes it. While he eats, I start to relax a little. Yes, he's a rat, but he's cute. I mean, in a rat kind of way. I try to assemble his house again.

"I'm Rocky. Who are you?"

"I'm Gabrielle."

"Sorry I had to get rough, Gabrielle. It's not easy being

a rat in New York City. But I'm working on something. I got dreams—big ones!"

"Really? What's your dream?" I ask.

"No, I'm not telling you. It's a secret."

"Okay," I reply as I add more layers of trash for the new roof.

"Okay! Okay! Geez! You badgered me enough—I'll tell you! I'm gonna be a rabbit."

"Um . . . a rabbit?"

"Yeah! Everybody loves those guys! Humans give them treats, let them live in their homes, and even pet them. No one has ever petted me. And let's face it: I'm adorable! But soon that will change!"

"How will you do that?" I ask.

"By thinking, moving, and existing as a rabbit. I'm almost there. Look!" He stands in front of me, clears his throat, and gets down on all fours. He lowers his face and looks up at me as if he's a doe-eyed rabbit. He's not. He still looks like a rat.

"Um . . . yeah, that's very rabbit-like." I know it's wrong to lie, but I don't want to break his little rat heart.

"Thank you; there's no need to clap," he says.

"But I'm not clapping—oh. Okay." I start to clap, and he bows.

"Where are you going at this time of night?" he asks.

"I'm meeting someone."

"A witch."

"Yes! How did you know that?"

"A witch's power is strongest at midnight. That's why

humans call it the witching hour. So, which witch are you meeting?" He starts to laugh uncontrollably. "Get it? 'Which witch'?" he says as he rolls on the ground with laughter. When he finally stops, he says, "I'm sure you can tell I do some stand-up comedy on the side."

"Oh, yes. And you're very good."

"Thank you. Now, what's the name of the witch you are here to meet?" he says, and takes a huge bite of his candy bar.

"Lady Lydia."

Rocky spits out his food and almost chokes. "You're going to see Lady Lydia? No! She's wicked. More wicked than all the other witches."

"She has something I need."

"What does she have?"

"Something that will make the kids at school like me."

"Don't they like you already?"

I didn't plan to cry. I didn't even plan to tear up or anything. It just happened.

"Gabrielle, tell me. What's wrong at school?"

"No one likes me. They all make fun of me because of my accent. They call me names. They tell me to go back to my country. I just want them to be my friend. But that will never happen if I don't change and become more like them. The witch says she can help me do that."

"Don't trust her."

I look at my watch; it's only three minutes until midnight.

"I'm sorry, I have to go, Rocky," I say. I take off running. I hear Rocky shout after me, "Gabrielle, no!"

The wind drowns out Rocky's voice. If he's still yelling, I can't hear him. I look at my watch—it's almost midnight, so I run faster. It's so easy to get lost here, the snow makes it hard to see well, and the night sky isn't helping at all. Luckily, I've been to this park before with my family. I know that just past the clearing of thick trees, there's a small stream that makes its way underneath the bridge. Now, where's the stream?

Wait, I see it!

I follow it, and it takes me to the meeting place. It was dark before, but now it seems as if the darkness has grown. The air has gotten even colder because of the water. I zip my coat to the very top and warm my hands in my pockets. It doesn't help.

I try to think about something warm: the midday sun on my back as my mom and I carry food in a basket on our heads from the market. I can almost feel the sunlight hit my body.

"Hello, Gabrielle. I'm so glad you decided to come."

I jump at the sound of Lady Lydia's voice filling the darkness.

"No need to be scared," she says. She whispers something to the ground, and a flame appears at once, giving us light. "There, that's better, isn't it? Now we have light and warmth. Would a bad witch do that?"

"Well, no . . . I don't suppose so."

"Exactly. I am nothing if not a sweet, kind woman who

aims to help lost little girls like you—children who have come here from far away and want to fit into their new home. I want to help you with the teasing, the loneliness, the relentless struggle of trying to fit in."

"How can you help me?"

"With this," she says as she extends her hand to me. She's holding a black and gold box. "Open it."

My stomach is jumping up and down again.

Not now, stomach!

"If I open it, does that mean I am agreeing to something?" I ask.

"No. For us to make a deal, you will have to say the words. So, go ahead, open it."

I look at the box. My heart is beating so fast that it's gonna jump out of my chest at any moment. I'm frozen, not sure what to do.

"You came all this way, dear. You might as well see what I have for you . . ."

Okay, Gabrielle, you can do this. Just open the box. And if it's something awful, like a dead raven or a beating heart, you can run away—fast!

I step closer. The wind wails, the snow whips all around, and the fire dims. I prepare for the horror that the box could hold. I take another step.

Lady Lydia says, "That's it, come closer . . ."

I take the final step, place my hand on the box, and open it.

"A mango?"

"It's not just any mango; it's a Carabao. It's the sweetest mango in the world."

The mango has been sliced into three perfectly equal, juicy slices. The warm, sweet scent fills my nose and makes my mouth water.

"It smells delicious."

"Yes, and it tastes even better," she promises.

"But how can it help me?"

"You make a wish, and then eat a slice of mango. Whatever you wish will come true."

"Do I have to eat the whole slice—can I just take a small bite if it's a small wish?"

"No, for your wish to come true, you have to eat the entire slice of mango."

"So I would get three wishes?" I ask.

"Exactly."

I narrow my eyes and study the witch carefully. "And what will it cost me to make the wishes?"

"Nothing—well, almost nothing."

I fold my arms over my chest like my parents do when they are about to ground me.

"Lady Lydia, don't try to trick me. If I make a wish, what will it cost me?"

"Okay, fine. You will lose some small, insignificant thing. Something you won't miss at all," she says, avoiding eye contact.

"Like what?"

"You may lose a strand of your hair or maybe a sock. There's really no way to say for sure."

"Then I can't say yes to this deal, not if I don't know what it will cost me," I reply. I start to walk away.

She suddenly appears before me and stands in my way. "Gabrielle, you misunderstand my intentions. As I've said before, I've helped many kids in your situation. But don't take my word for it. Here, see for yourself," she says as she waves her hand over the stream. On the surface of the water appear dozens of kids laughing and playing, from different parts of the world.

"You helped all of them?" I ask.

"Yes. This stream is a reminder of the good that I have done. I call this the home of a thousand laughs because, well . . . look at them. They are all blissfully happy, thanks to me. So, how about it, dear girl? Do you want to join them? Do you want to be happy? Or do you want to keep your life the way it is?"

"I . . . I need to think about it."

What if Stephanie was here? What would she tell me to do? I know, she'd take my hand and drag me back home. She'd say it's crazy to make a deal with a witch. She'd be right. She's always right about this kind of stuff. But Stephanie's not here. And I need friends . . .

"Here, perhaps this will help," the witch says. She waves at the water, and suddenly the scene on the surface changes. The water is now reflecting me at school. I'm at school, playing with kids from my class. But they aren't laughing at me. They are laughing with me. We're all playing together. My chest aches. I want that. I want that so much.

"That can really happen?" I ask.

"Yes! You can wish your accent away. That alone will help you get friends."

"And all I will lose is a small thing that I didn't want anyway?"

"Yes, something very small."

"I guess that's fair . . ." I reply as I look inside the black box again.

"Now, there's just one small, tiny thing I have to mention."

My stomach flips again. I ignore it. "What is it?"

"It took some time to create this mango. I worked hard on it. And, well, it's only fair that I get something out of it. Right?"

"I guess . . ."

"So, if you eat all three slices, I get to take something from you—your essence."

"My what?"

"Exactly! You don't even know what it is. Don't worry about the details. So, we have a deal?"

I look down at the image in the stream. The kids at school, they like me. They actually like me! I know it's just a spell Lady Lydia cast, but it could be real—it could all be real.

I feel something tap on my ankle, hard. "Ouch!" I cry out and look down—it's Rocky. He shouts up at me. "Gabrielle, no! Don't do it!"

I shoo him away. He continues to yell as he climbs up onto my shoulders. He pleads with me. I turn to him. "Rocky, I know what I'm doing. I have a plan."

"Don't do it!" he yells.

"I told you, I have a plan. I will only eat one slice; I'll only make one wish. That way, she will never get my essence — whatever that is."

"Do we have a deal?" Lady Lydia asks.

Rocky starts to argue, but I put my finger over his mouth. "Yes, Lady Lydia. We have a deal."

I grab the box and race back home as fast as I can. I'm so happy; I don't even feel the cold anymore. Rocky is following me. He's mad at me for making a deal with a witch, but I promise him again that I know what I'm doing. I sneak back into the house. I'm glad that everyone is still asleep, because I don't want to use my wish to get back in the house without being seen. I climb through the window and wave goodbye to Rocky. I get into bed and smile to myself. Tomorrow, everything in my life will change . . .

CHAPTER SIX
Almost Like Magic

THE SUNLIGHT BEAMS DOWN on my bed. I sit up quickly and get ready for school. I'll make my wish right before I get to the bus stop. That means the faster I eat breakfast, the faster I can go make my wish.

"Gabrielle, chew," my aunt says.

"Yeah, why are you in such a hurry to get to school? I heard they tease you even worse than before," Kayla says.

"Is that true? Is it getting worse?" my uncle asks as he adds yet another coat to the two he already has on.

"Don't worry about it. I can handle it," I reply.

"Gabrielle, this is very serious. We have to go down to your school and talk to your teachers about this," my aunt says.

"Would that mean missing work?" my uncle asks, his face wrinkled with concern.

In a Haitian family, missing work is almost a crime. If you lost a leg or an arm, they would still expect you to go to work. My mom said she went back to work an hour after giving birth to me. I'm not sure that's true, but what I do know is that, like with school, missing work is unacceptable.

And if my uncle has to take time off work to help me out at school, he'll lose money. His job won't pay him for that day. And the same will happen with my aunt. I would feel so bad if they had to give up a day of work just for me. Also, them coming to my school would only make the kids tease me more. Besides, I have already fixed the problem— I hope.

"They were bothering me at first, but I think that's over with. You don't have to come. If it's still a problem, I'll let you know, okay?"

My aunt and uncle exchange a look. I hold my breath. After a silence that lasts forever, my aunt says, "Okay, but if the bullying doesn't stop, tell us right away, promise?"

"Promise," I reply. I quickly swallow the last of my oatmeal, kiss the twins goodbye, and head out the door.

Once I am across the street from the bus stop, I pause. If this doesn't work, I don't know what I'll do. I can't take any more teasing. And I can't take being so lonely all the time.

"Well, aren't you gonna cross the street?" someone says behind me.

"Hi, Rocky," I reply without having to look down. "What are you doing here?"

"Well, you helped me rebuild my house, which makes us friends. And even though I don't think you should trust the witch, I hope you get what you want. I hope you get to belong."

"Really? Thank you."

"Did you make the wish already?" he asks.

"No, not yet. I'm about to," I reply as I look around for a private place.

"Let's go there!" Rocky says. I follow him to a small alleyway across the street from the bus stop.

I open my bookbag and take out the black box. Inside the box are three glowing slices of mango. Rocky looks worried. "Rocky, I don't need socks. So it's okay to make this wish, because I won't really be losing anything important."

"Yeah, I guess you're right," he says, with his eyes glued to the mango slice in my hand.

"I wish to lose my Haitian accent and speak perfect English." I put the mango slice in my mouth and bite down. It's even sweeter and juicier than I thought. I feel the burst of flavor in my mouth, and my cheeks get warm. Suddenly, a chill passes through me. I don't know what it means; maybe it means the wish is happening.

"How do you feel?" Rocky asks.

"Um . . . okay, I guess," I reply.

"You want to try speaking English with me?" Rocky asks.

"You're an animal, you guys understand every language," I point out. "I want to try on someone who only speaks English."

Actually, I want to start with the word that is hardest for me. The word that Tianna and her dolphins always tease me about. I walk out of the alley and march up to the kids waiting in line for the bus. And in a small, uncertain voice, I squeak out one word: "bathroom."

Oh. My. Gosh.

It came out right! Normally, it always comes out "baf-room." But this time it came out right!

There was no awful, thick accent. It came out in perfect English!

I run back over to Rocky, who's hiding behind a mailbox. "Bathroom! Bathroom! Bathroom!" I shout, laughing. Rocky and I are dancing together. I'm so happy, I'm pretty sure our feet never touch the ground.

"All right, I'm gonna go back over there and try other words."

"Which words?" Rocky asks.

"All of them."

"Whoa . . ."

I run back toward the bus stop. And the first person I speak to is the girl who tried to help me up when I fell.

"Hi, I'm Gabrielle. What's your name?"

Every word that comes out of my mouth the better my English sounds. No trace of my accent. The girl looks shocked. "Hi, I'm Carmen. I wanted to say hi before, but I wasn't sure you'd understand me."

"Why not?" I ask with a big smile. "I speak English very well. Actually, I'm kind of an expert."

"Wow, you learned English so fast! It took me forever!"

"Where are you from?" I ask.

"Mexico. How about you?"

"You know, here and there. Hey, you wanna sit together?"

"Yeah, sure," she replies. We get on the bus and sit side by side. The other kids are shocked and listen in as Carmen and I have a conversation. No one is more stunned than Tianna and her dolphins. She glares at me as the other kids start to join in our conversation. She's boiling mad that no one is teasing me. I smile. I look out the window of the bus and wink at Rocky as the bus drives away.

———

The wish worked even better than I thought. I'm speaking English like I was born in America. I don't know most English words; I know them all. And for the first time since coming to America, I have a friend. Carmen is nice and very funny. She tells me about sneaking up behind her mom and taking cookies. She's so good at it that her mom thinks they have a ghost.

When the bus lets us out at school, I rush inside with my new friend. Someone calls out my name. I turn around.

"Hi, Mrs. Bartell."

"Gabrielle, your accent is so much lighter now."

"I've been practicing so I could improve," I reply.

"You've more than improved. Your English is perfect," she says, raising her eyebrows.

"You know me, practice, practice." I giggle nervously. I feel a bead of sweat form on my forehead. My heart has decided it would do better outside my body.

"You're sweating and fidgeting. Are you okay?" she asks.

I nod. And then, to really sell it, I smile.

She says something in a different language; it sounds familiar but I don't know what she actually said. I stare back at her.

She repeats it again. Nothing. So she tries it in English, "Gabrielle, I want to show you something."

"Oh, okay."

"Didn't you understand when I said it to you in Haitian Creole?" she asks in English.

"Yeah, of course I did. I just wasn't paying attention." I grin and tell her to lead the way. She makes a face but then starts down the hall.

I follow her; we go into the library. At the center of the room, there's a giant gold and silver map on display. It's in a large frame and has writing on the edges.

"A map?" I ask.

"Yes, we just got it in this morning."

"It's nice. I gotta go!" I reply, but before I can take off, she stops me.

"This map gave me an idea. In a few weeks, it will be Culture Day. That's the day that all the students get to talk about where their families are from. Some kids write a report, but others do presentations. I thought when it's your turn to go on stage and talk about Haiti, you could use this map to show people where Haiti is located."

"Um . . . I'm not sure."

"There could be more to your presentation than this map. You could bring in a dish from Haiti to share with the class. Maybe sing the national anthem. Or show us old family pictures. What do you think?"

"Mrs. Bartell, that's nice and everything, but . . . I don't want to do a presentation for Culture Day."

She sighs and looks down on the floor. I don't understand why she's reacting this way. What kid would want everyone to know they are new to America? I just want to fit in, and now that I have, no way I'm standing up in front of the school and announcing to everyone that I'm not from here.

"Mrs. Bartell, are you mad at me?"

"Oh no, of course not." She smiles sadly and asks me to sit at the reading table along with her. "I know how hard it can be to fit in. And I just wanted you to know that fitting in doesn't mean you throw away who you are."

I sigh and roll my eyes.

"That's rude, Gabrielle!"

"I'm sorry, Mrs. Bartell, I really am. But when the kids know you are from a different place, everyone picks on you. Culture Day sounds more like 'torment day.' Sorry, I'll do the homework, but I won't get up there and speak. And I definitely won't be using the giant map. Can I go now?"

She sighs again. "Yes, you can go."

"Thank you!" I grab my stuff.

"Gabrielle?"

"Yes?"

"I miss it."

"What?"

"My accent. It took years to go away, and when I was little, that's all I wanted it to do—go away. But sometimes I find myself missing it. I think you're going to miss your accent too."

"No, never."

"You lost it rather . . . quickly. It's almost like magic."

I laugh—too hard. "Mrs. Bartell, you're so funny! How can anyone use magic to lose their accent? That's crazy."

"Yes, it would involve seeking out a witch, and we both know that's not a good idea. Don't we?"

"Y-y-yeah," I reply, then I swallow hard and start to walk away.

She calls out, "Gabrielle, *fé atansyon*."

I turn back. "What?"

"That's Haitian. It means be careful," she says slowly.

"Oh yeah. I knew that. I just didn't hear you. Bye, Mrs. Bartell."

———

For the first time since I came to America, my classes are easy. I don't sit in the corner hoping to fade into the wall. I don't silently pray that the teacher doesn't call on me to read out loud. And best of all, I don't feel like everyone is making fun of my accent. Instead of dreading class time, today I am excited about it.

"Who would like to read the first passage from your homework assignment?" my teacher asks. My hand shoots up in the sky. My teacher is surprised. "Gabrielle, you would like to read for us out loud?"

"Yes, Ms. Stevens. I would."

She nods to me. I stand up.

"You don't need to stand up," she says.

"Yeah, I kind of do—this is a big moment."

She smiles and says, "Well then, by all means—please carry on."

I open the book and read out loud. I don't have to chase my words and beg them to come out correctly. I don't have to work triple hard on my pronunciation. Everything just flows together beautifully. When I am done reading, the teacher stands there with her mouth open. The class nods. Carmen tells me I did a good job.

When we go out for recess, I don't just play games with the other kids—I lead, because I understand the rules now. I play with Carmen and the other kids in my class, and no one is laughing at me. I finally belong.

We're in the middle of a game of tag when suddenly one of the students shouts, "The candy lady opened her window!" Everyone in the yard is excited. The kids gather in small groups and crawl through a hole in the fence.

"Where are they going?" I ask Carmen.

"Didn't you hear? The window's open!" she says, jumping up and down.

"What does that mean?"

"It's March, spring is almost here. That means the candy lady opens her window and sells treats," she says.

"What kind of treats?"

"She has every candy you can think of, and she has a thousand Popsicle flavors. Even the flavors I get when we go on vacation to Mexico. Her Popsicles come in a small plastic bag. When I get them, I tear into them with my teeth and suck on the ice until my brain freezes." She laughs.

"Okay, let's get some," I reply, but then I remember something and my heart sinks.

"What is it, Gabrielle?"

"I didn't bring any money with me," I reply.

Someone behind me starts laughing. I turn around, and it's Tianna and her awful dolphins. Don't they ever take a day off from being mean?

"What are you laughing at?" I demand.

"You. You don't have any money. And I know the reason why," Tianna says with her nose in the air.

"That's not true. I do have money. I have a lot of it. But I left it at home," I mumble as my stomach churns.

"No one in your house has money. You're from Haiti. Everyone there is poor. Carmen, you have to go to the candy lady by yourself. Your new friend is too poor to come with you."

The dolphins begin to laugh. I fold my arms across my chest and scowl. I rush toward her, but Carmen stops me. "Don't listen to Tianna."

"But she's always picking on me. And now that I speak perfect English, I can argue with her and have a billion words I can use."

"You'll get in trouble," Carmen warns me.

"Come on, girls; let's go see the candy lady. We'll get a big bag of candy. Or maybe two," Tianna says smugly. They follow her through the hole in the fence.

"Come on, let's go," Carmen says.

"I can't. I told you I don't have any money."

"But I do. We can find something to split."

"No, it's okay. You go ahead."

"Gabrielle, if I didn't have money, would you share with me?"

"Well, yeah."

"So, it's only fair for me to share with you. Now hurry, before the window closes," she says. We crawl through the hole in the fence, then sneak over to the red brick house.

"Are you sure we aren't going to be seen by the teachers? They're right over there," I point out.

"Ha! That's never gonna happen. Not on my watch," someone says behind us.

We turn and come face to face with a kid named Getz. His real name is Melvin, but everyone calls him Getz. Why? Because whatever you need, he can get it for you—so long as you can pay his price. Getz wears a gray fedora and trench coat—every day. It's odd, but the kids have gotten used to it by now.

"There's no way the teachers would tell on us," Getz says.

"How do you know?" I ask.

"You're new around here, so I'll let you in on a little secret, kid," he says with a cocky smile. He signals for us to come closer. He leans in and whispers, "It's a well-kept secret, but the fact is, teachers love the sweet stuff too, can't get enough of it.

"Yeah, sure, they act all grown-up when we kids are around—broccoli this and vitamins that—but it's all an act. Teachers have a sweet tooth. And I'm the one who gets them what they need: Nutter Butters, Ding Dongs, or Twinkies. I get them all. And so long as they get their treats, there won't be any trouble," he says proudly.

"Getz, can you really get anything your customers ask for?" I ask.

"Haven't you heard my motto?" he asks.

"No," I reply.

"You want it—I Getz it. Here, take my business card," he says, handing us two white cards with his name on it.

"Um, thanks," Carmen says.

"No problem. There's a ten percent discount if you refer a friend," he shouts as he takes off.

Carmen nudges me—it's almost our turn at the window. I get a good look at the candy lady in the window. She's plump and perfectly round, like a ball. Her skin is dark and radiant like the night. Her eyes sparkle, and her puffy cheeks glow.

There's a beautifully colored wrap on her head that's as high as a tower. She's wearing a pair of earrings shaped like colorful parakeets. There's a matching necklace dangling from her neck, with the initials *MM* on it. The candy lady leans forward and talks to the boy who's next.

"Henry, I told you before, there will be no more chocolate until you get a note from a dentist."

"But my dentist says my teeth are fine."

"Okay. Smile," she says; the boy smiles. He's missing six teeth. "Next!" the candy lady says.

"Aw c'mon, candy lady. Please?" the boy begs.

"Oh, all right, all right. Here," she says as she reaches inside a basket near the window. She hands him a green apple.

"Very funny. What am I supposed to do with this?" the boy says, shaking his head as he stomps away.

The girl in front of us places her order—three peppermint-chocolate balls and a strawberry Popsicle.

"All right, that will be fifteen dollars and fifty cents," the candy lady says.

Everyone in the line gasps. Candy has never cost that much, no matter how big a bag a kid gets. There's no way.

"Fifteen bucks for candy?" the girl says, stunned.

"No. The candy is fifty cents. But the box of laundry detergent your mom has to get to take out the stains you leave on your shirt after eating the candy costs fifteen dollars."

I look the girl over, and the candy lady is right. I can make out everything she has had to eat so far today: The dark brown, glossy syrup stain from the waffles or pancakes. The bright orange spot she dripped on herself while drinking her orange juice, and the shiny sparkle of sugar from the bag of Sour Patch Kids she had earlier.

"You're charging me for the detergent?" the girl demands. "That's not fair!"

"Neither is your mom staying at the laundromat until nightfall. Now, you want me to come down on the price, I will. Only if we can come to some kind of understanding."

"Fine. What are your terms?" the girl asks.

"You don't purchase anything that drips, sticks, or stains," the candy lady announces.

"Aw, man. What does that leave me with?" the girl asks.

The candy lady turns her back to us and then swivels around holding something. "Behold, the world's first stain-free Popsicle!"

"It's an ice cube on a stick!" the girl says.

"That's right. And it's all yours. Free!" the candy lady says as she hands the ice pop to the girl.

The girl groans and storms off.

"All right, who's next?" the candy lady asks.

"We are," Carmen says.

"You two still have most of your teeth?" the candy lady asks.

"Yes," we reply in unison.

"Well, then I guess it's okay," she says. "I've got just the thing for you." She hands Carmen a small bag of lollipops.

"What flavor are they?" I ask.

"It's my favorite—mango with chili. Here, try one." She hands me one. I put it in my mouth, and right away, the spicy-sweet flavor floods my mouth.

"This is so good!" I reply.

"What kind of candy do they eat in Haiti?" Carmen says.

"You're from Haiti?" the candy lady asks.

"Ah, yes. Kind of," I reply with my eyes on the ground.

"Look people in the eye when you talk to them. And especially when you are talking about your birthplace, young lady. I've been to Haiti. Good people. Strong. Smart. Kind."

"Yeah, I guess," I reply.

"Sorry, but we gotta go," Carmen says as she pays the lady.

As we make our way back, I can't help but feel like we're being watched. I turn around and catch the candy lady looking at me in a strange way. Like she can see right through me . . .

———

When school is over, I take the bus and sit next to Carmen. She has an older sister who is a teenager, just like my cousin Kayla. We laugh about how boy-crazy they are and how much makeup they wear. The other kids join in, and soon, the whole bus is buzzing with stories and laughter.

When the bus gets to my stop, Carmen and I say goodbye and make plans to sit together again the next day. As soon as I step off the bus, I find Rocky waiting for me by the lamppost.

"So, how did it go?" Rocky says before I can greet him.

"It was perfect! Everything was perfect! Oh, Rocky, you should have seen it—they liked me. And all I had to do was lose my accent!"

"Well, that's not all. You also lost something else, remember?"

"What do you mean?" I ask.

"Well, Lady Lydia said each wish would cause you to lose something."

"Oh yeah, like a sock or something I don't care about . . ."

"Exactly. So, do you still have both socks on?"

I look down at my sneakers, and both socks are on.

"Maybe one of the socks in my dresser is gone. Let's go look," I tell him as I run toward my building.

I enter the apartment and have Rocky go around back and get in through the window. It turns out we didn't need to do that—no one's home yet. My aunt and uncle are still at work. The twins are at daycare and Kayla is probably hanging out with her friends. She's probably practicing kissing boys with a pillow. I saw her do that once—teenagers are so weird.

I enter my room, and Rocky is on the windowsill waiting for me. I go over to my dresser drawer and look through my socks.

"Well?" Rocky asks.

"All my socks are here. Even the ugly ones my uncle got me with the pictures of bacon and eggs."

"Your uncle got you food socks?" Rocky says.

"I know, I know. He just likes pictures of food on clothes. He thinks it's funny. He got my aunt a sweater with pasta on it. It's awful. My aunt keeps 'accidentally' throwing it in the trash. But whenever she does, he finds it."

"Okay, so all your socks are here. Then what did the wish cost you, if not a sock?" Rocky says.

"Well, the sock was just an example. The wish could have taken my pajamas. Or maybe one of my dresses."

"I saw a horror movie once, and a monster took the little girl's toes."

Rocky and I lock eyes. The fear we feel is bigger than the sky itself. Could it be? Do I still have all my toes?

"I would feel my toes being taken, wouldn't I?" I ask in a weak whisper.

"There's only one way to find out . . ." Rocky says as he

looks down at my feet. I swallow hard, sit on my bed, and take off my shoe.

"Ready?" Rocky asks.

"Ready," I reply. I hold my breath, close my eyes, and slide my sock off my right foot. Then I open my eyes.

Five toes.

Phew!

"Now the other one," Rocky says.

"Okay, one more time," I reply as I take my other shoe off. Rocky looks on, his eyes wide with fear. I slide my left sock off and—five toes!

"Yes!" I shout.

"Who has all her toes?" Rocky asks.

"I do!"

"Who does?"

"I do!" I laugh.

Our celebration comes to an end when I hear someone at the door. My family's home.

"Do you want me to go?" Rocky says.

"No, you stay here; I'll go say hi and see if I can get you something to eat."

"Food? Yes, like what?"

"Maybe a nice piece of cheese?" I offer.

"Well, I am training to be a rabbit, but I suppose rabbits eat cheese, so yes."

"Okay, be right back."

I rush out to the kitchen, where my family has gathered.

Everyone is talking and joking around as they help put away the groceries. In a panic, I run back into my room and close the door behind me. My heart is beating so fast that I put my hand over my chest, hoping to slow it down.

"So, where is it? Where's the cheese?" Rocky says.

"I know what the wish cost me."

"Oh no, the wish took the cheese? Why? Why so cruel?" Rocky says as he throws himself down on the windowsill and takes out a handkerchief to dry his tears.

"No, the wish didn't take away your cheese," I reply in barely a whisper.

He studies the shock on my face. "Gabrielle, what's wrong?" he says as he gets closer.

"My family is out there talking to each other."

"And?"

"And I couldn't understand a word they said. Earlier today I couldn't understand Mrs. Bartell, but I thought I just wasn't listening. It wasn't that. I can't speak or understand Haitian Creole. Rocky, the wish took away the language of my home . . ."

CHAPTER SEVEN
Witch Hunt

I TRY OVER AND OVER AGAIN to understand the things that my aunt and uncle are saying. It's no use. It's like they are speaking some kind of alien language. Rocky helps me look up Haitian Creole in the *Encyclopedia Britannica*. My aunt and uncle can't afford to buy us the whole set, but thankfully, we have books that cover up to the letter *H*.

"'This language is a mix of eighteenth-century French and West African languages,'" I read out loud. "Maybe I only lost some Haitian, but kept the French part?"

So, Rocky tests out my theory. Luckily for us, he speaks every language. He speaks French, and I don't understand a word. We try for over an hour to get me to speak Haitian Creole, but nothing works.

"Oh no . . ."

"Maybe you can start over. And learn to speak Haitian from the beginning," he says.

"Okay, let's try it," I reply.

Rocky gets up and says, "I am here to teach you Haitian Creole."

"Yes, okay. I'm ready."

But I'm not ready. I didn't realize it before, but Haitian Creole can be a hard language to learn. I slump down on my bed. It's no use. My native language is gone for good. Rocky tries to cheer me up, but I'm not in the mood.

"Are you sure a magic trick won't help?"

"I don't think so," I say.

"I can pull a rabbit out of a hat for you."

"Really?" I reply.

He runs over to my dresser, gets inside a baseball cap, then jumps out and says, "See, rabbit out of a hat!"

I try to smile, but I can't. "Thanks for trying, Rocky."

"I'm sorry."

"It's not your fault. How am I going to talk to my family now? It's one thing to practice English, but to not speak Haitian Creole at all? And not being able to understand them? They are going to know something is up! And then I will have to tell them about doing a deal with a witch. Then they'll send me back to Haiti for misbehaving."

"Maybe I can speak for you. I'll whisper to you what to say, and you just repeat it."

"That could work, Rocky, but wait—how can you be around all the time? People would see you. They'd notice that I'm using a rat as a translator. It would never work." I sigh and lower my head.

"What if they don't know I'm there? What if I become invisible?"

"Rats can be invisible?" I ask.

"Don't be silly, of course not. But it just so happens that I know who owns a glass squid cape."

"Glass squids?"

"Yes, glass squids are the magicians of the sea. Their skin is completely see-through. They can hide anywhere. They aren't nearly as cute as rabbits, but they are useful."

"And your friend has a cape made from them? Who's your friend?"

"A turtle I once helped get back on his feet—literally. That guy was on his back for days before I came along. He owes me one."

"A glass squid cape. Honestly, that sounds kind of gross."

"Maybe, but it will get the job done. Using the cape, I'll be around to translate for you and no one will see me—until we figure out a better way."

"I guess we don't have a choice. Can you go get it now?"

"Be right back. Act normal until then," he says as he scurries out the window.

Rocky comes back half an hour later, just as my aunt is calling to me. He sits on the windowsill with a small black cape that fits around his neck perfectly.

"I can still see you," I tell him.

He dips his hands into a glass of water on the windowsill and throws a few drops on the cape. He disappears right away!

"Rocky, it worked! I can't see you!"

My aunt calls up to me again. All I recognize is my name. I can't see Rocky, but thankfully, I can hear him.

"Your aunt said, 'Come to the phone—it's your mom,'" Rocky says.

Rocky and I make our way to the phone. I hold the receiver out far enough that he can hear what my mom is saying and say it back in English.

My mom's beautiful voice fills my ears. Rocky whispers what I should say. He keeps it short—I say *wi* and *non*, which mean "yes" and "no." That's it. That's all the Haitian I know.

My dad takes the phone and talks fast. He laughs. He's made a silly joke. He does that. But now I won't hear the jokes or get to roll my eyes because they aren't funny. And when the call is over, my mom signs off, saying "I love you." She says it in Haitian, and Rocky translates it for me. But I didn't need him to tell me what she said. I think "I love you" doesn't need translation.

When I am done on the phone, Rocky and I go back to my room. Rocky is excited that we got away with it, but I'm not as happy. Actually, I'm kind of sad.

"What's wrong?" Rocky asks as he takes off the cape.

"You did a great job translating, but it's not the same. I couldn't tell my mom about my day or hear about hers. When we get on the phone, sometimes she tells me a quick story, or she tells me who won the mango-eating contest this week. I'll never understand what she's saying ever again, without your help. Rocky . . . what did I do?"

For the next week Rocky has to follow me everywhere around the house. He says he's okay with it, but I feel bad, so I try to give him treats whenever I can.

Rocky says he likes staying over at my house because there's always a "show." He means there's always something crazy happening. Monday, Kayla and my uncle have an argument about which hair color is "respectable." My uncle says, "Only the hair color God gave you." Kayla says, "God made hair coloring. So, maybe he meant for humans to color their hair blue and pink." They only stop when my aunt calls out to them, letting them know dinner is ready.

On Tuesday, Kayla and my uncle argue about the rap music that she likes to play. They end up having a kind of battle to see whose music was better. He plays old-school Haitian and French songs, and she plays hip-hop. I think both types are too loud, but when they ask, I just smile. Rocky is having the time of his life. And as soon as the argument starts, he gets a chunk of cheese and settles in for "the show."

On Thursday, my uncle asks my aunt to make him a nice, hearty soup for dinner, because it's cold outside. So she makes my favorite soup, *soup joumou*. It's a spicy soup they make in Haiti with squash. My mom puts a lot of good stuff in it, like beef and potatoes. She also puts in vegetables, but they just get in the way, so I usually take them out.

My uncle tells my aunt how delicious the soup smells and thanks her for making it. He's right; it smells really good—almost as good as when my mom makes it. Kayla and I have to set the table while my aunt goes to the kitchen to get the soup. Suddenly, we hear two small voices shout, "Surprise!" Then my aunt screams and we hear the sound of glass shattering.

We race to the kitchen and find my aunt standing in a puddle of soup while the twins cross their arms over their chests and nod proudly—they managed to surprise us again. They hid under the kitchen sink and waited for my aunt to come and then popped out holding a dead mouse.

My uncle has had enough. He lightly swats the twins on their bottoms three times. I don't think it hurts them; mostly they look surprised. Their little mouths form Os and they pout.

"No more surprises, okay?" my aunt says.

"Okay," they reply in unison.

That night, we have pizza for dinner.

And while I'm stuffing my face with extra cheese, I tell my family that I will only be speaking English from now on so I can focus on my new life in America. Rocky tells me that my uncle says, "It's fine to focus on English. Since you were born in Haiti and went to school there, Haitian Creole won't fade from your memory."

I force a laugh. "Ha! A whole language fading from memory, that's . . . crazy!"

———

The next morning, before I go outside to the bus stop, I do the same thing I have been doing all week long—look for the red door in the lobby. But so far, there's no red door and no sign of Lady Lydia.

"It's not fair, Rocky. She should have said that I could lose something as important as my native language."

"Witches are sneaky," he says as we make our way to the bus stop.

"Well, she's not gonna get away with this."

"What do you want to do?" Rocky asks.

"I have to find the witch and get my language back. But I can't spend all day looking for her. I'll miss school."

"Don't worry, Gabrielle, I'll see what I can find out. I will meet you at recess. Hurry, the bus is here," Rocky says.

I run after the bus and get inside right before the door closes. I plop down next to Carmen, breathless and worried.

"What's wrong?" Carmen asks.

"You wouldn't believe me if I told you."

"Try me," she says with a mischievous smile.

"You'll think I'm crazy."

"I like crazy. Crazy sprinkle colors, crazy loud music, and crazy friends."

"That's right, we are friends . . ."

"Of course."

I think about it, and I remember how she tried to help me when Tianna made me fall on the bus. I remember her smiling at me even though I didn't know how to speak English back then.

"Okay, I'll tell you, but this has to be between us," I reply. I whisper the whole crazy story, and to my surprise, she actually believes me.

"I know a few witches in Mexico. Some good. Some not so good."

"They have witches there too?"

"Oh yes. It's not a good idea to trust one. And now your language is gone. How are you gonna get it back?" she asks.

"I'm gonna make the witch give it to me."

"Can I help?"

"Sure. How do you feel about witch hunting at recess?"

"I'm in!"

"Great! Let's meet by the double doors as soon as recess starts. Oh, and I'll introduce you to my other friend, Rocky the rabbit."

"You're friends with a rabbit?"

"No, I am friends with a rat who thinks he's a rabbit."

Carmen looks me over and whispers, *Ella es loca*.

I'm not sure what she's saying, but I think it's Spanish for "My friend is crazy."

———

When recess time comes around, the rest of the kids gather outside to play. Carmen and I sneak off and go back inside the school. I open a window so that Rocky can come inside.

"Did you find out anything?" I ask him.

"No, sorry. Hey, who's that?" Rocky asks when he sees Carmen. He scrunches his face and turns his nose up at her.

"I don't know how I feel about adding another member to our little team. I wasn't consulted," Rocky says.

"But Rocky, she can help. Her name is Carmen. Say hi," I say.

"Hi," he mumbles stubbornly.

"Hi! Wow, Gabrielle, I didn't know you made friends with a rabbit! He's so cute!" Carmen says as she winks at me.

"Me? A rabbit? Well, aren't you sweet . . ." Rocky says, pretending to be shy.

"I'd love to be friends, but if you don't want that, then okay," Carmen says, pretending to be hurt.

"Wait! I guess you can come along. I'm a rabbit, and we are very inviting creatures."

"That's great!" Carmen says. I whisper "thank you" as I walk by her.

"Where do we start?" Carmen asks.

"Let's start with the places I've talked to her around school. Down this hallway—let's go!"

We spend our recess looking for Lady Lydia in every inch of the school. It was so easy to find her before, but now, she's nowhere in sight.

"And just what are you two doing out of class?" Mrs. Bartell asks.

Both Carmen and I jump at the sound of her voice.

"It's recess," Carmen says.

"That ended ten minutes ago. You girls are late. You know better than to play around when you should be in class," Mrs. Bartell says, looking disappointed.

"We're sorry. It won't happen again," Carmen says.

"It's too late for that. You girls are going to be written up. We will send a note to your parents letting them know that you two have been horsing around."

Carmen and I look at each other in full panic. "Mrs. Bartell, it's not Carmen's fault," I say. "She was helping me find something I lost. Please don't send a letter home for her. It's my fault."

"Don't send a letter home for Gabrielle. She just wanted to find something she lost," Carmen says.

"And what is it you misplaced?" Mrs. Bartell says.

She looks over at me. I want to tell her right then and there, but I don't know how. How do I tell her that I lost my language?

"Gabrielle, what did you lose?" she asks again.

"Um . . . I lost my pencil set. It's my favorite."

"A pencil set?" she asks suspiciously.

"Yeah, it really meant a lot to me."

"Well, if it means that much, I assume next time, you'll be more careful with it. Right?" she asks.

"Right," I reply with my head down.

Mrs. Bartell looks at both of us. "You girls can go. There will be no letters home. But you have both been warned. No more playing. Am I clear?"

"Yes, Mrs. Bartell," Carmen and I reply in unison.

She signals for us to be on our way. When Carmen and I turn the corner, Rocky runs up to us.

"Was there any trouble?" he asks.

"No, but we were close. I wish we could get away as quick as you can," Carmen says.

"Yeah, we rabbits have it pretty easy," Rocky says.

"We better get to class," I say.

"What about the witch?" Carmen says.

"Rocky and I will keep looking after school. We should go inside now," I reply.

Rocky waves goodbye, and Carmen and I enter class. The teacher scolds us for being late. We take our seats, and the teacher continues the lesson. In the middle of class, I hear footsteps, but not just any footsteps. I hear the sharp click of pointy heels hitting the floor.

"I think Lady Lydia is outside in the hallway," I whisper to Carmen.

"Are you sure it's her?"

"Yes, I know by the clicking sound her heels make. It's her."

I raise my hand and ask to go to the bathroom. My teacher says no. She thinks I'm going to fool around in the hallways. I beg her, and she says that class is almost over and that I can wait to use the restroom. I turn to Carmen.

"The sound is fading. She's getting away," I whisper.

"I have an idea. Be ready," Carmen whispers.

I nod, and a few moments later, Carmen begins to sneeze. She does the best fake sneezes I have ever heard. Right away, the teacher asks her if she's okay. She plays it up even more and sneezes with her whole body.

"That's so good! I can't wait to tell Rocky what an expert performer you are, Carmen," I whisper.

"Gabrielle, go!" she says between sneezes.

"Oh yeah, right! Sorry!" I reply. And while the class is trying to tend to Carmen, I sneak out into the hallway, and it's just like I thought—Lady Lydia is strutting down the hall. I run and catch up with her.

"Lady Lydia, wait!"

She turns around and gives me a bright smile. "Hello, Gabrielle! I hear you've been looking for me. I think I know why."

"You do?"

"Yes, of course. You want to send me flowers for granting you a wish. There's no need. I'll get paid soon enough."

"What? No, that's not it. I'm not looking for you to thank you. You tricked me!"

She gasps loudly and places her hand on her heart. "Excuse me? I never trick anyone. I am hurt by your accusations, after everything I've done for you."

"You said my first wish would cost me a sock. But that was a lie. You stole my language!"

Her smile fades and her eyes are alive with sinister glee. "I didn't steal it. You gave it away!"

"No, I didn't!"

"Oh yes, you did. You knew that you would be losing something, but you didn't care. You wanted perfect English, and you got it."

"You said I would lose something I didn't care about."

"Yes, and you did."

"I care about speaking Haitian Creole."

"Did speaking Haitian Creole help you make friends? Did it help you not get bullied anymore? Did speaking your native language help make your life in America better?"

"No . . . I guess not."

"Exactly! So, who cares if it's gone? It was more trouble than it was worth. Now that you only speak English, your life is better. You have friends, you have fun, and you, my dear, are popular. Isn't that what you wanted?"

"Well, yes, but . . . I can't understand my family. I can't talk to my mom."

Lady Lydia mocks me and pretends to cry.

"Stop it! This is serious."

"Dear, I gave you the gift of the English language. It would have taken years to learn, but I gave it to you in a matter of minutes."

"But I lost—"

"The only thing you really lost was your old life. The life where no one liked you and no one could understand you. But now, thanks to me, you have friends. You have a life here in America. You're welcome."

"But—"

"Gabrielle, are you saying you want to undo your wish and get your language back?"

"Um . . . can I do that?"

"No, you can't. But even if you could, why would you? Your life is perfect now. No accent. No teasing. No problems. Again, you're welcome."

"I'm gonna wish for my language back."

"Oh dear, did I forget to mention this? You can't undo a wish. In fact, once you wish on a subject, you can't get another wish on that same subject. So none of your wishes going forward can have to do with language. Sorry. All you can do is create a new wish. But lucky for you, you have two perfectly good wishes left."

"You never told me that! Fine, but I'll learn Haitian Creole again, even if it takes years."

"Seems like a waste of time to me, but whatever you say, dear."

"And I'm not gonna let you trick me anymore. This is it! No more wishes."

"Are you sure about that?"

"Yes! No more. I'm throwing the last two mango slices away."

"You could do that, or you could wait until the party."

"What party?"

She laughs. I hate her laugh.

"What party?" I ask.

"One of your classmates is having a birthday party. She's inviting the popular kids. You speak perfect English now, so there's no doubt you'll be invited too. But I wonder . . ." she says quietly.

"Wonder what, witch?"

"Well, I'm just wondering if that's enough. Is speaking perfect English enough to get you to fit in?"

"Yes, of course it is!"

"Well, we'll have to wait and see . . ."

CHAPTER EIGHT
Problems

KAYLA WARNED ME that for Easter Sunday her mom would be waking everyone up early. I thought she meant at six or seven in the morning. I was wrong. My aunt wakes up the whole household at four a.m.! I groan and roll back onto my side. I have a lot more sleeping to do. But she shakes me again.

"Easter Sunday, no one sleeps! Everyone up! Church time," my aunt says in English.

"I think God is still sleeping, Auntie."

"No! Get up or we will be late!" My aunt's English is getting better.

"Can we go later?" I beg her as I rub my eyes.

"No. Shower. Now." She pulls the blankets off me. In Haiti we get up early on Easter too, but I guess my body forgot. And now, my aunt is here to remind me. "Gabrielle, let's go!"

I drag myself out of my room and head for the bathroom. I am not the only one unhappy with the time of day. I hear my uncle groan about this being his only day off. The twins are crying, and Kayla only has one eye open as she comes toward me.

"I'm taking a shower first. I got here first," I tell her.

She moves me aside and says, "I was born before you, so I got here first for everything." She enters the bathroom before I can stop her and shuts the door. I'm thinking maybe it's a good thing. Maybe I can get back to bed. My aunt sees me and says, "Do not think on it!"

I think she meant to say, "Don't think about it." But it's okay. I know exactly what she means.

My aunt moves around like a tornado as she gets the twins ready. They look adorable with their light blue bow ties and gray suits. My uncle wants to wear a funky tie. So he comes out of the bedroom with a tie that has ducks and taxicabs on it.

"Is my aunt gonna let you wear that?" I ask.

"I am a grown man. I can wear what I want."

My aunt walks past him, sees the tie, and says, "No." And right away, my uncle goes back into the bedroom to change.

We are about to head out the door when my aunt looks us all over. We all look pretty good in our Sunday best. All us girls are wearing dresses, even Kayla. She hates it and sighs every five seconds. But she looks beautiful.

The twins are still sleepy and leaning against the wall, hoping to get back to sleep. My aunt has on a flowing baby-blue dress and her hair is pinned up. She's wearing a large blue hat that covers most of her face. Rocky comes out of my room wearing a tie. I guess he didn't want to be left out. He puts on the cape and disappears.

Kayla warns me that the church service will go on forever. She's right. We enter the small basement church and stay there for about three years. Okay, less than that, but that's what it feels like. The pastor goes on and on and on. I tell Rocky he doesn't need to translate. He gladly runs out of the church and says he'll be back before the service is over.

A while later, the pastor's voice goes soft, and people around me begin to bow their heads. I guess that means we are near the end. Thank goodness. I think that God must be tired and wants to go back to bed, just like we do.

When the service lets out, we shake everyone's hands and mumble something. Rocky is not back yet, so I just nod but don't say anything. My stomach is twisting in knots. I'm so hungry that I could eat a whole chicken all by myself.

"Are we done? Can we go eat?" I ask Kayla.

"Yeah, and that's the best part. The church rents a banquet hall every year and has Easter lunch. This year it's right down the block."

My stomach hears the news and growls. Then my uncle's stomach growls too.

My aunt hears it and laughs. "We go to eat now," she says in English.

The whole church walks down the street together. We look like a small parade of large hats and pastel dresses. I linger behind, looking for Rocky. Thankfully, he shows up just in time so I can join the others.

"Where were you?" I ask.

"Had some stuff to do," he says as he puts on his cape and disappears.

"We're going to eat. I'm sure you'll find plenty of things to snack on."

I don't need to see Rocky to know that he's glad we're headed for a meal. I can hear it in his high-pitched, excited tone. We enter the banquet hall, and it's beautifully decorated with flowers, streamers, and balloons. They also have long tables with colorful pastel tablecloths.

We all take a seat, and the women in charge of the lunch serve us tray after tray of food. It's like everyone's mom went into the kitchen and came back with their best meal. There's sweet plantains, fried beef, pork, and rice and green beans. There's also rice and red beans, rice and black beans, rice and black mushrooms—Haitians like a lot of rice. They also pass out trays of salad and veggies. I try to get out of taking any, but my aunt shoots me a look, so I put some salad on my plate.

I bend down and secretly place food for Rocky under my chair. There are a lot of Haitians in Brooklyn, but this is the first time I've seen so many gathered in one place. It makes my heart ache that I can't understand what they are saying, but at least I can watch them talk and have a good time. I wish my parents were here. They'd have fun too.

I notice everyone falls into their groups. The men stick together and discuss the other religion they truly love and care about—soccer. The women gossip about how wrong it is to gossip, and the teenage boys are checking the girls out. The girls pretend they don't notice—but they do.

All around me there's conversation and laughter. I get to hear my uncle laugh and watch my aunt be the center of attention. They never really get to hang out and talk because they, like most Haitians, are working too many jobs to stop and slow down. But today, they have the chance. Even my uncle has the whole day off. I hated getting up early, but now I'm glad I did. Today I got to be back in Haiti again—or close to it.

———

My uncle was right, spring is late. We're two weeks into April and it's still pretty chilly outside. It's not as bad as when I first got here, but I still need a jacket to go outside. And to make things worse, it's been three weeks since I talked to Lady Lydia. She was right—Kim Ashland is having a birthday party. She has invited lots of kids from school. Everyone is talking about it. I haven't gotten my invite yet, but that doesn't mean I won't get one. I speak perfect English, so I'm sure it's only a matter of time before she hands me an invitation.

"What do you think of this dress for the party, Rocky?" I ask as I twirl around in my bedroom. The dress I'm holding up to the mirror is one of my favorites. It has palm trees and snow. Yeah, I know it's bizarre, but that's why I like it.

"It's nice, but ..." Rocky doesn't continue. He looks worried.

"Rocky, what is it?"

"You have your heart set on going to this party, but what happens if Kim doesn't invite you?"

"She will; I'm delightful. And I don't have an accent anymore," I remind him.

"Well, if she doesn't invite you, we have a bowling night every Tuesday downtown. You can come bowl with us."

"I didn't know you knew how to bowl," I reply.

"Well, I don't. Rabbits aren't great bowlers."

"Then why are you in a league?"

"The uniform really brings out my eyes."

My aunt calls out for me to come to the kitchen. I leave my room and head for the kitchen, where an elderly woman with dreadlocks and glasses sits in front of a plate of food. My aunt uses her broken English to introduce me to the woman.

"Mrs. Anderson, my niece is name Gabrielle."

My face gets warm from embarrassment. My aunt used the English words in the wrong order. I wish I could get my whole family something so they could speak English as well as I do now. But that would mean that they would no longer understand Haitian Creole, and I don't think they would want that. They would miss their native language too much. I miss it too—a lot.

"Hi, Mrs. Anderson."

"Mrs. Anderson lives two blocks away. We always take bus together," my aunt adds.

I smile, not sure what I'm supposed to say. Then my aunt

tells Mrs. Anderson that it's hard for me since I'm not from around here.

"Don't worry, Gabrielle," Mrs. Anderson says. "It's always hard to make friends when you first come to America. I have an idea. My granddaughter goes to your school; why don't you come over for dinner and the two of you can talk? She's my little angel, and I'm sure she'll help you out at school."

"Um . . . yeah," I say. "Okay. But I already have some friends."

"You do? That's good. But don't let them tease you. My granddaughter, thank goodness, never went through that phase. She's a sweet girl from Jamaica. And when she came here, she stayed just as sweet and just as nice as she was back in Kingston," Mrs. Anderson says proudly.

"She sounds so nice. What do you say, Gabrielle—you want to make a new friend?" my aunt asks.

"Yeah, sure. I guess," I say.

"Good! Next week, you and granddaughter come for dinner?" my aunt says. The two of them get all worked up about planning a meal that will be both Haitian and Jamaican. I sneak out of the kitchen and go back into my room.

"Okay, now where was I?" I ask Rocky.

Silence. I look around the room, and there's no sign of Rocky. We usually say goodbye before he takes off. I guess he had plans. I start to put my clothes in the closet and hear a knock on my door.

"Come in," I reply. Carmen opens the door; I smile at her

and start to show her my dress options. "Okay, what do you think? Too much? Maybe this white and green dress?"

"That's nice," Carmen says. "Gabrielle, there's something I need to tell you."

"I know what it is," I reply with my hands on my hips.

"You do?" Carmen says.

"Yeah, I know—I only have one good party dress. How can I get my aunt to get me a new one?" I ask.

"That's what I came to talk to you about—you won't need a new dress. I'm sorry. You're not getting an invite to the party."

I feel like someone punched me in the gut. My knees are weak. Thank goodness the bed isn't too far away. I sit on the edge of the bed quietly as all my hopes sink to the floor.

"Why doesn't Kim want me at her party? Hasn't she heard me speak? I can say even the hardest English words without stumbling. Listen: otorhinolaryngology, Worcestershire sauce, and here's a big one—lasagna!"

"That's really good, Gabrielle," she says as she sits next to me.

"Then why won't she invite me?"

"Well, I heard that . . . Never mind. Who cares? We can have our own fun here," Carmen says.

"Wait, what did you hear? Tell me, please."

"Tianna told her not to invite you because you won't fit in at the party because you're not American."

Rocky appears in the window. "Sorry, I had to step out for a second. I spotted a rat who owed me money. Hi, Carmen!"

"Hi, Rocky," Carmen mumbles.

"That's it!" I say. "I'm gonna confront Tianna tomorrow, once and for all!"

Rocky looks over at us and says, "Did I miss something?"

———

The next day, I take my seat in the cafeteria, next to Carmen. I take out the lunch my aunt made for me. Usually around lunchtime I'm starving. But today I couldn't care less about the food. My stomach is in knots, and it will stay that way until I have it out with Tianna. I see her enter the cafeteria, her dolphins close behind her.

I feel so many things all at the same time. I'm boiling over with anger, and yet my fingers are ice cold from nerves. There's a lump in my throat because I have no idea what to say, but my mind is racing with all the words I want to spit at her. I get up to go over to Tianna, and Carmen comes with me.

"You don't have to go with me," I tell her.

"Yes, I do. Friends have each other's backs."

We nod at each other and march over to Tianna.

"Yes?" she says innocently.

"What is your problem?" I demand.

"Excuse me?"

"Why did you tell Kim not to invite me to the party? What did I ever do to you?" I roar at her.

"Gabrielle, I did you a favor. I was looking out for your feelings," she says.

Carmen and I look at each other, confused. "You were looking out for me?" I ask, folding my arms across my chest like my mom does when she's upset.

"Yes, I was looking out for you," Tianna says.

"How?" Carmen asks.

"Gabrielle, you're nice enough, but you're not like us Americans. I mean, yes, you speak perfect English. But that doesn't change the fact that you're not American. You're from some poor, faraway country with no lights, no food, and you sleep in huts. What would you know about a party? I didn't want you to be embarrassed."

"You don't know Haiti and what my life was like back there," I protest.

"No, but I know you're not American," she says as she walks toward my table. She stands by the food my aunt made and studies it like it's a science experiment gone wrong. "Seriously, what is that?"

"It's rice and beans with goat meat."

Tianna says, "Goat! Ew, gross."

The other kids start to lean in and stare at my lunch.

"You never heard of chicken in your country?" Tianna says.

"For your information, we have chickens!" I shout.

"But only, like, once a year, right? The other times your family eats goats. And what else? Bears, raccoons? Wait—do you guys eat dogs? Oh my gosh, Gabrielle eats dogs!" she announces to the entire lunchroom. Everyone except Carmen begins to laugh.

Tianna shouts over the chorus of laughter, "That's why it's not a good idea to invite you to the party, Gabrielle. Kim has a dog—she doesn't want to walk into the kitchen and see you eating him for a snack!"

I do not tell my body to do what it does next. I don't give my fist a command. It moves on its own. And before I know it, I deck Tianna in the face—hard. She slumps down to the ground. But then she gets up and hits me.

"Fight!" someone in the crowd yells. It's Carmen and me versus the rest of the school. Food is flying everywhere. The crowd is out of control. The security guards rush over to us and try to pull us apart. By the time they stop the fight, Carmen has a bloody lip, I have a black eye, and both of us are missing a shoe.

———

"What were you girls thinking?" Mrs. Bartell demands as we enter the library. It's Carmen, Tianna, and myself. The rest of the lunchroom was forced to stay inside and clean up. They won't be getting recess for a full week because of the brawl. Mrs. Bartell snapped us up, and now all three of us are standing in the library waiting with our heads down.

"Gabrielle started it," Tianna says.

"That not true! She's been tormenting me since I got here," I declare loudly.

"She's just jealous that I'm from America and she's not. She's jealous of me and everything I have," Tianna says.

"Oh, please, no one is jealous of you—you're a lunatic!" Carmen responds.

"Okay, okay—that's enough!" Mrs. Bartell says. "You are all in trouble. We do not condone violence of any kind in or outside of this school. Is that clear?"

All three of us mumble, "Yes."

"And you, Carmen—" she begins.

"It's not her fault. She was just helping me," I protest.

"Gabrielle, is Carmen your friend?" Mrs. Bartell asks.

"Yes, she's my first friend in America," I reply.

"Then why do you keep getting her in trouble?" Mrs. Bartell says.

"What? I . . . I didn't mean to . . ." I reply as I look at Carmen's bruised lip. "Carmen, I'm sorry."

Carmen smiles sadly and shrugs a little.

"Carmen, I know you didn't start this, but going along with it wasn't right," Mrs. Bartell says. "You should have called a teacher. Or better yet, you two should have talked out the problem. We never use our hands. And for that, you will stay after school for the next week doing extra class assignments. Got it?"

"Yes, Mrs. Bartell," Carmen says.

"Good, and the next time I hear about you taking part in a fight, I will call your parents, young lady. Do I make myself clear?"

"Yes," Carmen says.

"Now go to the nurse's office and then head back to class." Carmen rushes off.

"And as for you two . . . what is the issue? Why do you dislike each other so much?"

"She hates that I'm from Haiti," I reply.

"Really, that's so interesting . . ." Mrs. Bartell says as she studies Tianna. There's a puzzled look on Mrs. Bartell's face. Tianna avoids her gaze.

"But that's not true, is it, Tianna? You don't have a problem with immigrants, do you?" Mrs. Bartell says.

"No," Tianna says.

"Good, I'm so glad to hear it. Now, I spoke to the principal, and he agrees—you two are in serious trouble. Tianna will be losing all her recess time getting the school ready for Culture Day. And as for you, Gabrielle . . . according to the kids in the lunchroom, you marched up to Tianna. That means you started it."

"But I—"

"No buts. I'm taking you to the principal's office. We will call your aunt and uncle and tell them the news."

"What news?" I ask.

"You're suspended from school."

———

My uncle is mad; his face is turning tomato red. And since he has dark skin like me, that's a very hard thing to do. And yet he's doing it—he's turning bright, shiny tomato red. There is a good chance his head might actually explode.

Rocky translates everything my aunt and uncle are saying in Haitian Creole. But to be honest, I don't really need the translation—anger, like love, is pretty easy to figure out, no matter what language.

"How dare you get into a fight?" my uncle shouts.

"How could you do this, Gabrielle? You know better than to be so reckless!" my aunt says. There are veins in her forehead that get bigger and bigger by the second.

"Do you understand how much sacrifice has been made so you could get to America and make a better life for yourself?" Uncle asks.

"Well, I—"

"Don't speak, young lady! Do not dare open your mouth!" I nod and remain quiet. But then he says, "What was going through your mind? Huh? What were you thinking?"

I don't say anything because he said not to talk.

"Answer me when I'm talking to you!" he shouts.

"But you just said—"

"Never you mind what I just said! Tell us what you were thinking!"

"She has been mean to me since I got there. And you guys don't care. You don't care how awful she made me feel," I blurt out before I can stop myself.

"Did she touch you? Did she hit you in any way?" my aunt asks.

"Well . . . no . . ." I reply.

"Then you should have just paid her no mind. Ignore her," my uncle says.

"That never works."

"Why didn't you tell us? We could have gone down to the school," my aunt says.

I roll my eyes and drop my head into my hands.

"Why didn't you tell us things had gotten this bad, Gabrielle?" my uncle asks. "When we asked you before, you said things were better."

"I thought they would be better, but ... Forget it. You don't know what it's like to be different and have everyone hate you for it. I was finally making friends and then ... she embarrassed me, and ... Just forget it." I make a run for my room, hoping to get there before I burst into tears.

"I did not dismiss you, Gabrielle," my uncle calls out.

I stop in my tracks, and the tears fall. I didn't want them to, but my body isn't really taking orders from me today.

"I know it's not easy being new in this country. But you have to find a better way to handle things than fighting. That's not the way you were raised."

"Yes, Uncle," I reply softly. He hands me a tissue.

My aunt hands me the phone. "It's time we call your parents and let them know what's been happening."

My heart stops. Just like that, it just stops beating. I feel an icy-cold wind rip through me. I would give anything, *anything*, not to make that call.

"Do I have to?" I ask.

"Yes, you do," my uncle says.

I start to dial. My mom picks up after a series of long clicks and strange connection noises.

"Mom" is all I can manage before tears flood my eyes. My uncle takes the phone from me and tells my parents about my suspension. Mom yells so loudly that the whole house can hear her. And thankfully so can Rocky, who translates for me.

Mom says, "We have all our hopes and all our dreams tied up in you. You are our better tomorrow. We work until our backs break and our fingers bleed. We do that so you can be someone someday and you waste that chance?

"Do you know how many children go hungry because their parents had to choose between school and groceries? There are girls—just like you—who will never know the inside of a classroom because their families can't afford it. You come to America, go to school for free, and you waste that chance? You waste that opportunity?"

"I'm sorry, Mom."

My dad takes the phone. "How can you break our hearts like this? How can you hurt us like this?"

"I wasn't trying to . . ." I say.

"Gabrielle, listen to me. Everyone makes mistakes. And although we're upset right now, we will forgive you. It's okay. But we need to know that you have learned from this and that you will behave."

"Yes, I have," I promise. They tell me they love me and want me to have everything they never did. Then they speak to my uncle once more, just before saying good night.

"I won't be any more trouble," I promise my uncle as we make our way back to my room. I'm glad Rocky is there, and he whispers what I should reply in return. But I kind of wish he didn't translate the last thing my uncle says to me . . .

"I hope you mean it when you say you will behave, Gabrielle, because while we love you and love having you here . . . if you cause any more problems, we'll have to send you back."

CHAPTER NINE
In the Dark

I LIE IN BED and replay the day over and over in my head. I try to change some of the outcome, but I know it's pointless, since it's a memory, not a fantasy. I try to think about where I went wrong. There are so many places that I'm not even sure where to start. I keep hearing my parents' voices on the phone. They sounded so sad and disappointed in me; it makes my heart heavy. I stare out the window aimlessly.

I hear someone enter my room. Maybe it's my uncle. Maybe he's changed his mind and is sending me back to Haiti tonight. I quickly sit up and wrap myself in my comforter. My mouth goes dry. What am I going to say to change his mind? What if I can't think of anything? What if this is it for me in America?

"Gabrielle," someone says.

"Kayla?" I ask.

"Yeah, it's me."

I breathe a big sigh of relief; Kayla generally sticks to

speaking English, so I won't need Rocky, which is good, because he's not here right now.

"Sorry. Thought you'd still be awake with everything that went down today," she says. Thanks to the light from the lamppost outside, I can make out Kayla's silhouette as she sits on my bed. She hands me something on a plate. It's hard to see what it is exactly.

"It's bread pudding," she says.

"For me?"

"Duh, you're the only other person in this room," she says dramatically. The room is barely lit, but it's easy to see the annoyance on her face. "Who else would I bring it for?"

"Well, it's just that you've never done anything . . . nice for me."

"Well, don't get used to it. I have a reputation to uphold, and I plan to do so," she says in a stern voice as I start eating the dessert.

"Thank you, Kayla."

"Yeah, yeah. Don't get all mushy."

"I won't."

I eat while Kayla remains quiet. It's like she's trying to gather words to say something, but all the words she's picked are . . . wrong. So she doesn't say anything at all. I know that feeling very well.

She sighs. She likes sighing. It's like her pastime. I think it's a teenager thing. I wonder if I can major in that in college. I'd major in sighing and minor in "like, whatever." Teenagers are a handful.

"So . . . yeah, that's what I wanted to say," Kayla concludes as she pulls on the sleeve of her pajamas.

"You haven't said anything—at least nothing I could hear."

"Argh! Fine, I will say it again . . . a little louder." She says something, but it's not louder. I look back at her with a blank stare.

"Kayla, I got my new friend in trouble, my parents are super mad at me, and your parents are close to sending me away. Thank you for the food, but if you came to make fun of me or—"

"I'm sorry."

"Wait—what?" I ask.

"I came here when I was seven. And it was really hard. Kids used to call me . . ."

"Call you what?" I ask.

"A . . . monkey. They used to say awful things about Haiti and about my family. I was in trouble all the time for standing up for myself. And then some new girl came to the school from another country, and they focused on her. That's the only way I was able to get any peace."

"They called you names?"

"All kinds of names. But then the new girl came. So, just wait for the new girl."

"I don't want to wait. And I don't want the new girl to be treated like I was, either," I reply.

"Yeah, it sucks. Look, the reason I came here was to give you an 'I'm sorry' bread pudding."

"Why are you sorry?"

"I don't get teased now, but as I said, I used to. I should have looked out for you. I could have taken some of the heat off you. I didn't. And I'm sorry about that."

"It's okay," I reply. We sit in silence for a few moments.

"The truth is even if Kim had invited you to her party, you wouldn't have been able to go."

"Why not?"

"My parents never let me go to a party."

"So you've never been to a party?"

"A few, but that's only after years of begging."

"Tianna said I wasn't American enough to go to a party. But I thought that since I speak good English . . ."

"Yeah, I get it," she says.

"Kayla, how do you know when you are American enough?"

She doesn't reply. We just sit there, in silence, two Haitian girls in the dark.

———

The threat of getting sent back to Haiti is like an ugly tattoo I didn't ask for and can't rub off. I'm afraid to breathe the wrong way or say the wrong thing. If I got sent back, my mom would cry forever. And my dad would try to pretend like it's okay, but I know he'd be devastated. How did I let things get so out of hand?

Oh yeah, perfect English . . .

Something tells me Lady Lydia knew that speaking English wasn't going to be enough to get me to fit in. But I went and wished for it anyway, and now, I still don't fit in. And I'm in more trouble than I have ever been in my life.

It's the next day, and I usually would be getting ready for school, but for the next three days, I will have to stay home. Rocky has found a cozy spot in the corner. That way, he's always there in case I need him to translate in the middle of the night. My uncle wakes me up at six in the morning. He tells me that there is no way I am staying at home. So he's taking me to work with him to help out. I wake Rocky up. He yawns and mumbles something about beauty sleep. Before we head out with my uncle for the day, I write a quick note to Carmen telling her how sorry I am she got in trouble. Rocky tells me her parents aren't happy with me.

"Yeah, no one's happy with me lately," I mutter.

"Are you happy with you?" Rocky asks.

"Well, if there's a 'Gabrielle is a good girl' parade coming to town, I'd be the only one in attendance. And even I would be late."

"Hey, at least you didn't make any more wishes," Rocky says.

"Yeah, there's that, I guess," I reply as I hand him the note for Carmen. "How is she?"

"Carmen's okay. She can't wait for you two to hang out again when you get back to school. But only if you promise no more fights."

"Yes, there will be no more fights. I don't really have anything to fight for."

"I know you're down, but try to find something today to make you smile—other than the fact that you get to hang out with me."

I smile. "That is the one bright spot, Rocky."

My uncle knocks on the door and says, "Gabrielle, it's time to go."

I can tell by his tone that he's not done being mad. I quickly get the rest of my stuff and prepare for what I'm sure will be a long, boring day.

The three of us take the train to one of my uncle's three jobs. Today he's working for the cleaning company. He tells me that every week they have a new place to clean, and this week, the company is doing additional cleanup for Shea Stadium.

We walk through a series of faded gray and blue walls under the stadium. We enter an office area, where my uncle says to stand outside and wait for him. He goes inside the office and I take a look around, careful not to go too far and make my uncle even more upset with me than he already is.

When he comes out, he says, "My boss is okay with you helping me out today. Just do what I say and don't wander off. Okay?"

"Okay. How can I help?" I ask.

"We are cleaning the top section. There are chemicals, and I don't want you to touch them. But you can put on these gloves and start picking up the trash in the seats, okay?"

"I'm on it!" I reply.

We get up to the top section of the stadium, and my eyes

are popping out of my head. My uncle watches me and smiles. "I know. It's really big, huh?" he says.

"It's more than big, Uncle—it's gigantic. Our whole village can fit in here. Actually, I think all of Haiti could fit here! This is amazing."

"Yes, the first time I saw it, I stared for a long time. My favorite thing was playing soccer when I was a kid. I could just imagine what it would be like to play soccer out on that field. It would be magic!"

"Mom told me you and she used to play soccer all the time when you were kids. She said that everyone in the village thought you'd be a professional soccer player by now."

He doesn't say anything, just looks far off into the distance, like he's watching a movie that only he can see. Whatever the screen is showing him, it's making him sad and melancholy.

"Uncle? Are you all right?"

"Huh?" he asks as I pull him away from the feature playing in his head. "Oh yeah, I'm fine. Let's get to work."

And for the next hour, we clean row after row of seats. He's working hard and fast. He's done this for so long, it's like he's cleaning with his eyes closed. There are other teams of cleaners joining us; they each take their own sections.

"Bending up and down like this is hard. My back hurts," I admit.

"You can rest for a while," he says as he gets back to cleaning yet another row.

"Do you ever run out into the field? Just to see what it's like?"

"That would be against the rules, Gabrielle."

"And you never go against the rules. I know."

He laughs. It fills the section we're in. "Your mom and I got into more than enough trouble when we were kids. She fell in love with a pet chicken and stole him right off someone's porch. Your grandmother almost went to jail for stealing a chicken she didn't even know she had. Your mother hid him under her bed."

"Did they find the chicken?" I ask.

"Eventually. Then there was the time when your mom and I thought we'd skip school and go to the beach with our friends."

"What happened?"

"We got caught. Your grandmother came down to the beach to look for us. We were in so much trouble; we knew she'd kill us. And I mean, seriously end our lives. My sister and I saw your grandmother marching toward us as we got out of the water."

"What did you do?"

"We ran back in the water. Your grandmother can't swim, so we made a plan. We were going to swim to America!"

"That's really, really far away. And you'd probably die."

"Death by sea was much kinder than at your grandmother's hand." He laughs.

"When you got home, was she mad at you two?"

"She beat our behinds real good."

"Wow, sorry."

"It's okay. We were stubborn. We swore we knew everything. The truth is, our mom—your grandmother—worked hard so that my sister and I could have a better life."

I look around at him bending over to clean one of a million seats, and he reads my expression. "You're wondering if my life is better? And your mom's life?"

"Well, yeah."

"It is better. I know that cleaning isn't a glamorous job, but it helps me put food on the table for my family. I feel proud to do that. The only reason I came to America was that I had a mother who wouldn't give up on me. She borrowed, begged, and stole. All so your mom and I could have a chance. And that's what it's about—giving your loved ones a chance at something better."

"And this is better?"

"Yes, because in America, you start out a cleaning guy, but nothing says you have to end up that way. That is why in a few months, I will start night school."

"You're going to school?"

"Yes. I will start taking classes, and your aunt too. It's not easy, but we will find a way to do it. Find a way to better ourselves."

Okay, so the day isn't as boring as I thought it was going to be. My uncle tells me more stories about him and my mom. Stories that I've never heard before. And as I help him clean up, I can see the younger version of him—wild, happy, and full of excitement.

When my uncle asks if I want a lunch break now, I gladly say yes. We go down to where the offices are located. We sit in the small lunch area off to the side and unpack the lunch my aunt made for us.

A few moments later, two men in suits walk past us.

As they are headed out the main exit, the first man, who's wearing a red tie, looks over at us and says, "Every day, more and more Haitians come here. They're everywhere now."

His friend says, "Yeah, I notice that too. And who knows what diseases they bring here with them? They need to go back where they came from." He shakes his head. His friend nods in agreement.

I look at my uncle. I know he'll be as angry as I am at what those two men said. But instead of being upset, he just smiles at the men and waves goodbye as they go.

———

Whatever fun my uncle and I were having goes away with lunch. He's working fast and working hard, but it doesn't feel like he's in a hurry to get it done—it feels like he's trying to keep his mind busy so he won't have to think about what happened with the two men. I've never heard anyone say something so hurtful and wrong. I don't understand how grownups can talk that way.

I get that kids can say awful things, but grownups are supposed to be better, right? Why were they being so mean to my uncle? Wait, were they just trying to be mean, or do they really think that about us?

"Should I talk to him?" I ask Rocky, who fits perfectly in the front pocket of my overalls.

"Huh?"

"Rocky, are you okay?" I ask.

"Yeah, sure. I just got some stuff on my mind. You know —rabbit stuff."

"Okay . . ."

"And yes, you should talk to your uncle. Those guys were pretty mean. I'll help." Rocky signals he's ready to translate.

"Uncle?"

"Yeah," he responds as he continues to work.

"You heard what those men said, right?" I ask.

"Gabrielle, finish up so we can go home."

"Okay, I can work and talk," I reply as I start picking up the surrounding trash. "Do they think that about us? I don't get it. I thought it was just Tianna. Can it be that everyone in America thinks badly of us? What did we do to them? Why, Uncle? I don't understand."

"You need to finish up. I want to go home."

"But what about those men? What about what they said?"

"What about it!" he roars, filling the stadium. The other cleaners look up at us. Uncle takes a deep breath and goes back to working.

"I'm sorry. I didn't mean to make you upset. I just think it's awful what they said about you. I wanted to do something —anything—to defend you."

"You want to do something for me? Stop getting in trouble. Go to school. Get an education, so you don't have to end up working for jerks like that. That's what we have been try-ing to tell you. America doesn't always love people who look like you and me. America can be just as bitter as she is sweet. You have to learn to swallow both—bitter and sweet. That's just the way things are." Rocky translates for my uncle.

"Why are those guys so mean?"

"Just forget about it and work. Aren't you hungry? We can go home and get dinner as soon as this is done."

I look at him, and I realize he's not at all like I thought he was. I thought he was this big, tall man, who worked hard and kept his family safe. But he's not. He's just the new kid on the block, trying to handle bullies, just like me.

"Stop it," he snaps.

"What?"

"Stop looking at me like that. How dare you judge me, you spoiled little child! You think being brave is confronting everyone; well, you're wrong. Sometimes the bravest thing you can do is keep your mouth shut."

"I didn't say anything."

"You think I don't know what those idiots think of me? You think I don't know how they see me? I ignore it because I need this job to support my family. So stop judging me!"

I look at my uncle. He can't make eye contact. I think back to the question I asked Kayla . . .

"How do you know when you're American enough?"

The answer is simple: we will never be treated or looked on as Americans—no matter how long we've been here.

CHAPTER TEN

Shout!

MY UNCLE ISN'T MAD at me anymore. I think it's worse; I think he might be ashamed to look at me. When we make eye contact at the dinner table, he looks away. I don't want him to feel bad. It's not his fault he works with people who are rude. I wish he stood up for himself, but that's not something I can force him to do. I just want him to know that I don't care what they say about him. I know that he's a hard worker and a good person.

When dinner is over, he doesn't hang around and play with the twins like he normally does. Instead, he goes to the living room and watches TV. He's watching soccer and tries really hard to focus on the game. I guess I really messed up by bringing up what those guys said.

"What happened with you and my dad today at work? Why is he so moody?" Kayla asks as we clear the dishes. I tell her what happened, and she says, "When he's moody, my mom gets moody too. I can't handle both of them having an attitude. So, fix it."

"How?"

"Start by going in to watch TV with him," she suggests.

"And then what?"

"I don't know; make it up as you go," she says, practically shoving me into the living room, then listening in the doorway.

"Hey, Uncle, can I watch the game with you?" I ask.

"You have chores—are they done?"

"Yes, all of them."

He looks me over and grumbles, "Yeah, I guess."

I sit down on the sofa next to him. I'm not sure if this is a good idea.

"Do you want something to drink? I can bring it to you," I offer.

"No, thank you."

"Okay. How about a snack?"

"No, I'm fine. Listen, about today . . . the yelling . . ."

"I know. I upset you."

"No, you didn't. Those guys did, and I yelled at you, but I should not have. You didn't do anything wrong. They did. And I did. I should have said something. I would have, years ago, but now . . ."

"It's okay."

"You forgive me?"

"Is there money in it for me?" I ask.

He laughs. "Not a dime."

"Then sorry. My forgiveness is only for sale."

"I'll remember that," he teases.

"Uncle, do you ever miss back home?"

"Every minute of every day."

"But we came here with a purpose—you and me. To give our families a better future. So that's what we're going to do —right?"

He studies me. "That's right."

"Hey, it's still light outside, and it's warm enough to play soccer. Me, Kayla, and Auntie against you and the twins."

"You think you can take us?" he asks.

Kayla from the doorway and I reply at the same time, "Um, duh."

———

The second day of my suspension, I go to work with my aunt. Like her husband, she didn't want me to stay home all day and relax like I was on vacation. I agree, but first I get her to promise to speak English the whole day so that she can practice. That way, I won't need Rocky to come with us.

My aunt is a home attendant. She looks after this elderly Jewish woman named Esther Adelman. She lives in Manhattan, the fancy part. She owns a two-story house and has the prettiest rugs I've ever seen.

"Mrs. Adelman, meet my niece, Gabrielle."

The woman reaches out to shake my hand. Her grip is fragile, as is the rest of her. She weighs very little. The veins in her hands are big, running along her arms. I'm fascinated with her eyes. They remind me of a flashlight submerged in water. They are dull but so intriguing.

Mrs. Adelman has shiny, curly silver hair and wears dark

red–rimmed glasses. There's a necklace around her neck that gleams when the sun's light hits it in just the right way. It's a star.

"I like your necklace," I tell her.

"Oh, you do?" she asks. "Well, thank you. It's the Star of David. It's a symbol of my faith. I'm Jewish."

"My aunt told me that. But to be honest, I'm not really sure what that means."

She smiles, and instantly she looks younger. "Come sit. I'll explain it to you."

"Gabrielle, don't bother Mrs. Adelman. Let her rest," my aunt says as she washes the dishes.

"No, no, it's fine. I love the young people. My husband and I used to tell stories to the kindergarten class a few blocks from here. Oh, children are so fun. Not as bitter as us old folks."

"Okay, but if you get tired, let me know, and I'll help you lie down and take a nap," Auntie says.

"Yes, yes, I will be fine," Mrs. Adelman replies. "Now, where was I?"

"Mrs. Adelman, you were telling me about being Jewish," I say.

"Oh yes, that's exactly where we were."

The afternoon goes by really fast. Mrs. Adelman tells me about her faith, shows me pictures of the people at her synagogue, and tells me how she met her late husband, Marty. We trade stories about life in our native countries and all the adventures we went on.

Then she tells me that she is a Holocaust survivor. I'm not sure what that means, and I ask her to explain. She tells her family's story with tears in her eyes. When my aunt comes into the room, she scolds me for making Mrs. Adelman cry.

"Nonsense. Tears are shed. That's life. I'm happy to have someone to share my stories with. You bring her back anytime, you hear me?"

My aunt smiles. "Yes, I will do that. Promise."

My aunt makes food for us, and we have it out on the balcony. It's so nice to look out at the view of Central Park.

"Auntie, we should have a view like that. Is it expensive?" I ask.

My aunt sees Mrs. Adelman and they exchange a look of amusement. I have no idea what I said that makes them do that.

"You could grow up and get a view like this, Gabrielle. You just have to work hard. That's all," Mrs. Adelman says as my aunt preps her medication.

My aunt turns on Mrs. Adelman's favorite soap opera. She records one episode a day from Monday to Friday. But she saves them until it's Friday. That way, she can watch all five episodes in one sitting. I groan to myself, because I know that stuff is boring. Or so I thought. The truth is, it's three hours later, and I'm glued to the TV.

"Did this Max guy really throw his own grandmother down the stairs?" I ask as I watch the screen.

"Yes, all so he can get his hands on her money," my aunt says during commercials.

"Well, as sexy as Max is, he can take all my money just as long as I get some alone time with him." Mrs. Adelman laughs. My aunt laughs too. I'm not sure I was supposed to hear that.

My aunt tells me to help tidy up the house and vacuum the living room. I do as she says. When we are done, it's time to go, but Mrs. Adelman insists that we stay for one more episode.

"This is my second viewing, and I'm telling you, you can't miss this next one," Mrs. Adelman says.

"We can guess what will happen. Tina and Max go down the aisle," I reply.

"Or do they?" Mrs. Adelman says. My aunt and I look at each other.

"Someone spoiled their wedding?" I ask.

"And you'll never guess who!" Mrs. Adelman says. That's all it takes for us to be glued for yet another hour.

Someone enters the house; I can tell it's Mrs. Adelman's daughter. There are pictures of her all over the place. She's pale, thin, and dressed in a skirt and jacket.

"Oh, I'm glad you're here, dear Ruth," Mrs. Adelman says.

"Hello, Mom," Ruth replies, and kisses her mother on the cheek.

"And this young lady is Gabrielle," Mrs. Adelman says.

"Why is she here? We're not running a daycare," Ruth says.

"She's only here for the day, and we were just leaving," my aunt says.

My aunt signals for me to grab our things so we can go. The fun and easy feeling in the room is gone, thanks to Mrs. Adelman's daughter.

"We were having a nice time, dear," Mrs. Adelman explains.

"She's on the clock. We're not paying her to sit and laugh with you."

"I never charge your mother after my shift is over. We just talk," my aunt says in a strained voice.

"Yes, well . . . I'm here now. You can go."

My aunt takes our stuff, and we head for the door. Ruth calls to my aunt once again. Argh! We were so close to escaping.

"Oh, by the way. I notice the toilet paper is being used rather quickly. I'd appreciate it if you were to bring your own in the future. You do understand, don't you?"

My aunt is about three seconds away from losing it, I can tell. And part of me wants to tell the lady off. But then I remember what my uncle said about putting up with things for the good of the family.

"Auntie, let's go before we miss our train," I plead.

My aunt takes a deep breath and says good night to Mrs. Adelman.

"Oh, and I have been meaning to speak to your agency," Ruth says. "They always send me people with poor English, and, well, I was hoping we'd moved on from that. Does your agency have anyone who was born here? Anyone who won't need their hands held the whole time. I mean, really. I just don't have time for it."

My aunt is grinding her teeth so badly that I can hear it. Mrs. Adelman puts her head down. I don't think she likes what her daughter is saying.

"If you don't want me to work here—" my aunt begins.

"Then call the agency," I add quickly. "I'm sure if they have anyone else, they will send them. But I hope you will call for my aunt again, because it's been a pleasure to spend time with your mother."

"I don't know. Maybe. My mom does seem to enjoy your aunt's company. We'll see," Ruth says dismissively. I rush my aunt out of the building, fearing her gaze alone will set the entire place on fire.

———

I sit next to my aunt on the train and give her some time to compose herself. We ride in silence for a moment, and then she laughs. But it's not a happy laugh. It's more . . . dark and sad.

"Are you okay?" I ask.

"No. No, I'm not."

"What can I do?"

"Be good in school. Get a good job—own your own business. When you work for other people . . ."

"Is this the first time she's been that way with you?"

"Ha! Ruth is a pest. She buzzes and makes you dizzy.

She's mean with her words, and very sneaky. She always try to replace me. But I care for her mom so much . . ."

"I didn't realize your job was so stressful," I admit.

"I've worked for people who think I will steal, so they follow me around in the house. The lady before Mrs. Adelman sold her husband's watch and said I took it. She told the agency to let me go."

"What? That's awful! How did they find out the truth?"

"Her husband see pawn shop receipt."

"Bet you felt better when she had to say she was sorry."

My aunt smiles and shakes her head sadly. "You're so young . . ."

"She didn't apologize?" I ask.

"No such thing. And the agency fired me anyway."

"They should have stood up for you."

"The world has some good people in it, like Mrs. Adelman. But there are always others that . . . they just think of us as criminals, or worse, they just don't see us at all."

"What do you mean?"

"I don't think I would be say I am stealing if I walked in there with a pretty white dress and pretty white skin to match."

"Your former client just thought she could blame you because—"

"Gabrielle, soon you will be a woman. And what a black woman needs to know—regardless of where you were born —is this: in America, your color walks in the door before you do. Always."

"Argh! How do you do it? How do you not go crazy?" I ask.

She beams from the inside as she looks up at the map on the door of the train. "I'll show you how I deal. But it's a secret. Just you and me, okay?"

"Yeah, sure!" I reply.

"Let's go!" she says, taking my hand and guiding us off the train once the doors open.

"Wait, this isn't our stop," I remind her.

"We have some time. It's your uncle's day to pick up the twins. Come on!"

Before I can say anything, she hurries me along. We walk out of the train station and end up in the last place I ever thought she'd take me—Coney Island!

We enter a wonderland of roller coasters, street performers, and circus sideshows. I've always wanted to come here, but the family has never had time. The bright lights and energetic crowd make this place even better than I thought.

"You come here when you're stressed out?" I ask.

"I come here to scream. It's better here than screaming at my clients. Gabrielle, I was really upset back there. I almost threw Ruth out the window. Thank you for saving me from getting mad. I can't afford to lose my job."

"You're welcome."

"Do you want to shout until our voices open up the sky?" she asks.

"Yes!"

I look around to see which ride we should go on first. Coney Island is known for its super-scary and super-fast roller coaster—the Cyclone. I know that's way too fast and crazy for my aunt, so I try to pick something else.

"How about the carousel?" I ask.

"No, Grandma! We came to scream and shout. We came to get out our stress, and there's only one way to do that," she says as she winks and signals toward the ride across from us —the Cyclone.

Yes! Yes! Yes!

We get on the ride and strap ourselves in. The announcer asks if we are ready, and the crowd of passengers cheers. The roller coaster takes off, and my aunt and I hold hands as we rise to the top. The ride pauses, giving us a chance to brace ourselves. We look at each other, our eyes widen, and the car descends at top speed. We scream like wild, crazy lunatics. It's beautiful.

CHAPTER ELEVEN
Pure

ON THE THIRD AND FINAL DAY of my suspension, I babysit the twins. They drive me crazy and make me chase them all around the apartment. Thankfully, it's finally time for their favorite show, *Muppet Babies*. They sing along with the theme music and yell at me if I dare block the screen. What's even better is that there is a double episode, meaning I have more quiet time.

I go to my room but keep the door open in case the twins need me. I look in the mirror and the person looking back at me is very . . . Haitian. I have big, thick braids, brightly colored clothes, and last year's sneakers. How do I fix that? I want to be American. I want to look like they look.

I pull out the white plastic bag I hid in the back of my drawer. Inside is a box with a picture of a black girl with long, smooth, straight hair. American hair. I sound American—now it's time I started to look American.

I hear a knock at the door. I run to get it before the twins get cranky. It's Carmen. I let her in and hug her tightly. I feel like I haven't seen her in forever.

"How did you get away?" I ask.

"My sister is hanging out with her friends, so she couldn't wait to drop me off here. But I promised that I wouldn't get in trouble, so no witch hunting tonight. Okay?"

"Deal," I reply.

She says hello to the twins. They don't respond.

"Are they even alive?" Carmen teases.

"Hang on," I reply. I step in front of the TV screen, and right away they scream and cry.

"Okay, so they are alive," Carmen says.

"Come, I want to show you something."

Carmen enters my room, and I show her the box.

"What do you think?" I ask.

"Your family said you could perm your hair?"

"They never said I *couldn't* perm it."

"Seriously, just once, can't we eat pizza and look at cute boys in a magazine? Why does every meeting with you require an alibi and bail money? Can we pretend to be responsible for one night?"

"I'm being responsible by not making a second wish. The first wish made me lose something really important, so I won't wish again—even though I'm really tempted."

"So you're gonna perm your hair?"

"No, you're gonna do it, Carmen."

"What? Oh no! No way!"

"Why? You told me your oldest sister owns a hair studio. You've watched her work for years. You know how to do it. And I also remember you telling me that you have done perms for people."

"No, not people, a doll. Okay? That's not the same thing."

"Okay, fine. Then let's have your oldest sister do it."

"She won't touch you without a parent present."

"Then we are out of options," I reply, throwing my hands up in the air.

"No, we have another option—you stop being so crazy."

"What's crazy about changing my hair?"

"Your hair is fine."

"That's easy for you to say—your hair is like silk. It flows, it bounces, and you can run your fingers through your hair like on TV. That's a very American thing!"

"I like your hair. I liked your accent. I like you! Why isn't that enough?"

"Because it's not!"

Carmen shakes her head sadly and just looks at me. I turn away, not wanting her to see me cry. She puts a hand on my shoulder.

"It's not always easy for me, either. Sometimes people say mean things to my dad when he's working. They drive by his construction site, and when they see he's Mexican, they ask for the boss. They never think my dad *is* the boss. And even after he tells him, they still don't believe him.

"I was on a bus once, and some guy stepped on my mom's foot. She complained, and he told her to go back to her country, like we didn't belong here. And my sister came home crying once because some kid asked her why Mexicans are so lazy. It broke her heart, because she really liked the guy. And last year, someone spray-painted on my locker a word I'm not even allowed to say."

"All of that really happened?"

"Yes. But I'm not going to let it make me do bad or crazy things. I want to be around people who like me. People I don't have to pretend for. People like you. So please stop this."

"You have your family here. And my aunt and uncle are great, but my parents are still in Haiti. They are counting on me to be good. And if Tianna or anyone else keeps teasing me, sooner or later, I'll get in a fight again, trying to defend myself.

"That means I will be sent back to Haiti. But if I don't have anything for them to tease me about, I won't have a reason to fight. If I can be American, I will have no trouble, no problems at all."

"Gabrielle . . ."

"I know, I know! It looks like it's about my hair and my clothes, but it's more than that. I have to fit in to stay in this country. I have to do whatever it takes to make me like everyone else. You don't get it because your entire family isn't counting on you like mine is. Carmen, I'm all they have. I have to make this work. Please. Help me."

"I like you the way you are, and I won't help you change that. I'm sorry," she says as she walks out of my room.

"Carmen!" I shout.

She leaves the apartment.

I want to go after her, but I have to stay with the twins. And anyway, what would we say to each other? We're just on different sides, I guess. I look at the perm box and decide it's the only way to go. And I will do it myself.

———

The twins can't stop laughing, and neither can Rocky, for that matter. I guess that's what happens when the person standing in front of you has a huge bald spot.

"It's not that bad, right?" I say, mostly to myself.

It's hard to hear my voice when the twins' laughter drowns me out. I don't know what I did wrong; all I know is that chunks of my hair are coming out in my hands.

Rocky wants to be supportive. But first I have to get him to stop laughing. The kids know about Rocky. In fact, they talk to him when their parents aren't looking. They don't think there's anything weird about a talking rat who thinks he's a rabbit. But a bald girl in the middle of the living room they find very, very funny.

"Rocky! Stop laughing! You guys too!" I demand.

Rocky's rolling on the floor and can't catch his breath.

"Maybe you should try that thing that humans have—oh yeah, a wig. That's it! Get a wig! Oh, get one like Tina Turner. You know, that lady with that song—'Love Has Everything to Do with It.'"

"It's called 'What's Love Got to Do with It.' And this isn't that bad. I can fix it. Maybe if I put a bow on it or tie a scarf . . ." I play around with what's left of my hair. It's no use. Everything I try looks horrible. And every time I touch my hair, even more falls out.

Rocky finally gathers himself off the floor. Meanwhile, the twins are still pointing and laughing. I scoop them up one by one and put them in their room. They begin to get fussy, so I give them their favorite coloring book and a pack of crayons. It works. Soon they are too busy coloring to notice I'm leaving the room. I head back to the living room, where Rocky is still trying to behave himself.

"Let's not give up. There has to be a way to fix my hair."

"Call Carmen and see if she can help."

"I can't, Rocky. She told me not to do this," I say.

"Gee, why would she say that?" Rocky replies.

"Really not a good time for joking."

"Okay. I have an idea, but I'm not sure you'd be open to it."

"I'm willing to try anything!" I reply.

"How do you feel about circus life? You'd fit right in!" He roars with laughter.

I sit down at the table and look at myself in the mirror. My aunt and uncle will see this and then say, "It's time to go back to Haiti."

"I just wanted to be . . ." I sigh and swallow my words.

Rocky sits on the table and says, "I'm all out of laughter. How can I help?"

And that's when it hits me: there's only one person

who can help me. I go to the kitchen and get a nice chunk of cheese for Rocky. I need him to be in a good mood for what I'm about to tell him. I hand it to him, and he starts to eat.

"How is it?" I ask.

"Yummy! Thank you. Sorry I laughed at you. That wasn't cool," he says as he continues to chip away at his food.

"No problem. Do you remember when I went to my uncle's job?" I begin. "I thought that when I grow up, after having lived in America for years, I'd be seen as an American. But that's not true. Even when I'm a grownup, people will still look at me differently."

"You don't know that for sure," he points out.

"I do. I saw it happen at my uncle's job. They said mean things about him. It didn't matter that he was an adult or that he had been in America for a long time; they were still rude to him."

"That sounds awful. What did your uncle say to them?"

"Nothing. He didn't want to lose his job. The same thing happened to my aunt. Her client is really sweet, but her client's daughter is a nightmare. She talked down to my aunt and said these really terrible things. I don't want to grow up and have my life be like that. I thought things would get better by the time we grow up, but no, the bullying and torment keep going forever. Well, that is, unless you have what it takes to make it stop."

"How do you plan to make it stop?" he asks. I don't reply. He reads the expression on my face. "Oh no. Don't tell me you're thinking of making another wish," Rocky says, his eyes practically leaping out of his head.

"Just a little one!" I promise as I take the box of mangoes out from the back of the closet.

"No!" Rocky says as he grabs the box with the mango slices and runs out the window with it.

"Rocky, wait!" It's too late. He's off and running. I follow him out the window. Once he's on the ground, there's no keeping up with him. I race down the block, trying to catch up, but it's no use.

I run back into the house and get another piece of cheese from the kitchen. I place it on my windowsill. Soon, I see a pair of skinny claws and feet trying to sneak up to the plate of cheese undetected.

"Hi, Rocky."

"Darn it! That's not fair. You know how I feel about cheese."

"I do. That's why it worked."

"Fine, but I won't tell you where I hid the box," he says, his hands behind his back.

"Is it behind you?" I ask.

"Maybe. Or maybe it's hidden deep inside a secret lair at the top of the Himalayan Mountains."

"Or . . . it's behind your back."

"Yeah, that's another possibility. Guess we'll never know."

"Rocky!"

"All right, all right. Here," he says, taking out the box from behind his back.

"Thank you."

"But you shouldn't make another wish. That's a very bad idea."

"She already took my native language, so that's basically it. There's nothing else she can really take from me."

"Gabrielle, don't do it."

"I won't make three wishes and give her my essence. This is my second and final wish. This wish isn't just for me. If I fit in, then I won't get in any more trouble. That means I won't get sent back to Haiti for bad behavior. Enough talk. It's time."

I lift the mango up and bring it to my lips. "Sacred mango, make me one hundred percent pure American."

CHAPTER TWELVE
Apple Pie

I WAKE UP TO A BIG SURPRISE—my hair has grown back overnight. And this time it's straight and long. I turn my head from side to side, and guess what? I can whip it around, just like in the TV commercials. I run my hands through my hair and smile.

I look in my closet and see all the top-name brands. I look under my bed, and there is a row of new sneakers, just for me. I rush to take a shower and get ready. Today is the day when I become what I have wanted to be since I got here— American.

I don't even bother looking around to see what the wish took from me. The wish can have whatever it wants now that I get to be like everyone else. I go inside the kitchen and find breakfast already on the table; it's strawberry Pop-Tarts and milk. And on the counter is a box of Lunchables. Yes! There is no way to get more American—bologna, chips, and a juice box.

I shove the Pop-Tarts into my mouth and look through

the kitchen cabinets. There are so many new things in there my aunt would never ever buy: Kraft Mac & Cheese, Mr. T Cereal, and strawberry Nesquik. I look inside the fridge, and it's stocked with all the things I've always wanted to try: meatloaf, apple pie, and mashed potatoes.

This is it—this is a dream come true!

"Okay, how bad is it? I'm afraid to look," Rocky says as he appears in the kitchen window.

I smile. "Everything's great! You can open your eyes."

"Your hair . . ."

"I know, it's pretty, right?"

"Yeah, but I liked it the other way too."

"The other way made me different. I don't want to be different."

"Wow, you got a lot of food here," he says.

"I know! Any food that was in a commercial is right here in the kitchen. I'm gonna try them all as soon as I come back from school."

"I know you're excited, but will your family eat any of this?" Rocky says.

"Oh yeah, we used to eat an American meal once in a while. Like when I first came here."

"Yeah, but now they will only eat American food. All the stuff your aunt used to make Haitian food is gone."

"That's okay. We don't need Haitian food."

"Okay . . . so, what did the wish take away from you? You're not missing an ear or a toe or anything?"

"Nope, everything is perfect."

"Well, almost perfect."

"What do you mean, Rocky?"

He looks around the kitchen and then down the hallway where the bedrooms are.

"Gabrielle, where is your family?"

———

We look all over for my family. We look in the house, around the building, and down the street. We widen our search and look for more than ten blocks. We find nothing. I call the school; Kayla didn't show up. I call the daycare center, and they say my aunt didn't drop the kids off this morning. The last step is calling my aunt's and uncle's jobs. They tell me what everyone else has already confirmed: my family is nowhere to be found.

"Rocky, we need to find the witch. I know she's behind this."

"I have an idea about where we could find her. Maybe she's under the bridge like she was before," Rocky suggests.

We run to the park as fast as we can. Rocky is ahead of me, but I'm not too far behind. With every step, my heart hurts. How could I let this happen? What have I done to my own family?

When we get under the bridge, I call out Lady Lydia's name, but she doesn't appear. We spread out and look around, desperately seeking any sign of her. Rocky calls out to me and tells me to come over to the edge of the stream.

"What is it, Rocky? You found her?" I ask.

"No, look!" he says, motioning toward the surface of the

water. I look down into the stream that Lady Lydia called her "home of a thousand laughs." But this time, there is no laughter coming from the kids in the stream. Their bodies aren't bright and alive with joy like they were before. They are sickly, pale ghosts screaming at us in a hundred different languages.

"What are they saying?" I ask Rocky.

"They are saying, 'Please help us,' in every language."

"Every language?"

"Yes, except Haitian Creole. I don't hear any Haitian Creole," Rocky says as the cries get louder and louder.

"Rocky, look closer. They are trying to get our attention," I say as I get closer and closer to the kids. One of the boys is using his fingers and hands to convey a message to us. "I don't understand what he's saying."

"He's deaf. He's signing to us." Rocky watches the kid's hands. He's signing quickly, and with every movement, he's more and more frantic.

"Rocky? What's he saying?"

"He says, 'You are the last one.'"

"What does that mean? I don't understand! Rocky, ask him what he's talking about."

Rocky gets close to the edge of the water and signs to the little boy; he responds to Rocky by making the same hand gestures over and over again.

"What did he say, Rocky?" I ask. But Rocky isn't the one who responds.

"He said, 'Behind you.'"

A chill travels down my body as her breath hits the back

of my neck. My stomach flips, my knees lock, and my heart pounds inside my chest. I am terrified, but I am also livid. I whip around to face her.

Lady Lydia waves her hand at the stream, and it instantly glazes over. The kids are frozen under the water. They stand eerily still and look up at us with vacant eyes.

"Where are they, you heartless witch? Where's my family?"

"Really, dear, it's rude not to say hello first. I thought your parents would have taught you manners."

"Answer me, witch! What did you do to them?"

"I didn't do anything. You did. You wanted them gone, and I did as you asked. And now, you're here crying about it. Frankly, I'm a little tired of you making wishes and then complaining when I give you what you want."

"That's not true. I never wanted my family to be taken away."

"You said you wanted to be 'pure American.' Clearly, you wanted to erase all trace of your Haitian past. And, well, your family is part of your past. So, I got rid of them. You're welcome."

"You know that's not what I meant," I shout.

"Well, it seems we have misunderstood each other," she says.

"And what are you doing to the kids in the stream? They are trapped under there, aren't they? Is that what happens when I make the third wish? I will become trapped in the stream too?"

"The kids in the stream made deals with me. It didn't work

out well for them, but there's still a good chance for things to work out for you. How would you like to be the most popular kid—not in school, but in all of Brooklyn? I can make that happen. Just use your third wish."

I flash back to the roller coaster ride with my aunt, sharing bread pudding with Kayla, playing with the twins, and hearing stories from my uncle. They were there for me. And even when I messed up, they still loved me. And although they don't have a lot, they took me in and took care of me.

"No! I don't want to be popular or even fit in anymore. I just want my family back. And you better give them to me, now!"

Lady Lydia laughs and looks me in the eye. She whispers in a menacing voice, "Dear, you have no idea how long I've waited for you."

I think back to what the boy in the stream said. "I'm the last one," I say to myself.

"What does that mean?" Rocky whispers.

"I don't know, but I think it's important. And I think Lady Lydia really needs me for something," I say as I stare her down. "Well, whatever you are looking for, you won't find it. I will not help you do whatever it is you're trying to do."

"You're saying you want all of this to stop?" she asks.

"Yes! And I want my family back."

She shrugs and says, "Then wish for it, dear. And it will happen. Wish for them to return, and all of this will be over."

She waves her hand, and the black box I keep at home

appears in her palm. She opens it and takes out the last slice of mango.

"Here, take a bite. Help your family." She holds the mango out to me. I look at it but don't come closer.

"Gabrielle?" Rocky says when I don't make a move.

"Look at her eyes, Rocky. She doesn't just want me to take a bite; she *needs* me to take one. Something's wrong. If I bite that mango, something bad will happen."

"But Gabrielle, something bad has already happened. You've lost your native language and your family. Maybe you should make the wish and make everything better again," Rocky says.

"You can save them, Gabrielle. You can save your family. Take a bite," Lady Lydia says in a soft, hypnotic voice. I lean in closer. The scent of the mango pulls me in.

Maybe I should take just a small . . .

"No!" I reply. "Not gonna happen, lady!"

"Argh!" she roars angrily. "You eat this mango and save your family right now! Or else—"

"Or else what?" I say.

"I will open up portals through space and time and hurl them into it. Each one in a different portal. They won't have you there with them; they won't even have each other. They will be lost to time and space. Now eat!" she says.

"No."

She waves her hand, and a large crack appears under my feet. The ground splits open, and I fall into the gaping hole. I quickly grab on to the nearest tree branch, but it's not going to support me for long. I can feel it slipping from my fingers. I climb up just as Lady Lydia splits the ground open wider. I scoop Rocky up and take off running.

She summons the winds and the tree branches to come to life and ensnare us. We barely manage to dodge them as we run away. We hear Lady Lydia's voice in the wind.

"You'll eat that mango, or you'll never see your family again."

———

We make it out of the park with our lives but not much else. I'm covered in dirt and debris thanks to almost being swallowed whole by the ground. Rocky isn't looking any better.

"What now?" he says.

"We need help. I know who to ask. I just hope she's still my friend. Come on, let's go!"

Rocky and I hide in the bushes just outside of Carmen's math class, waiting for her to enter. I take a peek in the window. Carmen enters, sits down, and takes out her books. She catches a glimpse of me and screams her head off!

"Ms. Hernández! What is it?" her teacher asks. I quickly duck back inside the bushes.

"A bug. I thought I saw a bug, but it wasn't . . . a bug. It was a leaf."

"Well, be that as it may, that's no reason to cause us all to lose our hearing, now is it?"

"Sorry, Ms. Dove. Can I go to the restroom, please?" Carmen asks.

"You may. And maybe you'll come back with a more composed version of yourself?" the teacher replies.

"Yes, Ms. Dove," Carmen says as she heads out of the class.

I race around to the front of the school, careful not to be spotted by our security guard, Gordon. He's, like, one hundred years old and spends most of his shift sleeping in his chair. An army could have marched past him, and he wouldn't wake up.

I make my way to the girls' bathroom, the one nearest Carmen's math class. She enters and her jaw drops as she sees us.

"Gabrielle, what happened? I looked for you on the bus this morning. I couldn't find you. What happened to your hair? And why are you covered in dirt? I can't leave you two alone for one second."

"Hang on," I reply. I look under all the stalls. "Okay, we're alone."

"What's going on?"

"My family is gone. My uncle, my aunt, Kayla, the twins —everyone is gone."

"Are you serious? What happened? Who took them?" she asks.

I tell her everything.

"Did your parents in Haiti disappear too?" she asks.

"No. I called and heard their voices. They are okay. It's only my family here in America."

"Okay, don't panic. We'll find that twisted little witch. And we'll force her to take us to your family."

"Thank you for helping me. I'm sorry I didn't listen to you before."

"It's okay. No time for that now. We need a plan."

I try to pull myself together and focus on getting my family back safe and sound. Carmen is right. We need a plan.

"First, I think we should find out exactly who we are dealing with," I say.

"But we already know—it's Lady Lydia," Carmen says.

"What did the boy mean when he said, 'You're the last one'? Who exactly is Lady Lydia? How did she become so powerful? And more importantly, how do we stop her? All the things that I should have asked before," I say to myself.

My face falls, and I look at myself in the mirror.

"I'm not sad about how awful I look now," I say. "I'm sad about how awful I acted. I knew better than to make a deal with a witch like Lady Lydia. But all I cared about was making people like me. How could I have been so dumb?"

"You're not dumb. You made a mistake. But friends help friends fix things. So let's try, okay?"

"Thank you, Carmen."

"Sure."

"No—thank you for everything. You were nice to me from the beginning, and I didn't need the wish to make us friends. You were already my friend, and I should have been better with our friendship."

"Yeah, you're kind of a major pain," she teases. We laugh together.

"Carmen, I can't lose them. I can't lose my family."

"You can't think that way. Let's focus: Lady Lydia is the enemy. And we need to know as much as we can about our enemy. It's the only way to defeat her," Carmen says in a deep, commanding voice.

"Where did you learn to talk like that?"

"Our family plays a serious game of laser tag every year when we go camping. My mom and I are the Hernández laser tag champions three years running."

"That's cool. And . . . a little scary."

"Is there anyone we know who might be able to tell us anything more about Lady Lydia?"

"Well, Mrs. Bartell said something about magic when my accent went away," I reply.

"Do you think she was just joking?" Carmen says.

"No. Mrs. Bartell is Haitian. We never joke about witches."

"So she might know something. That's good. Let's find out as much as we can. Then figure out a way to take Lady Lydia down and get your family back."

CHAPTER THIRTEEN
Home

CARMEN HELPS ME CLEAN UP as much as she can. We wait until school is over so we can talk to Mrs. Bartell. We knock on the library door, and Rocky stands on the windowsill.

"Hello, girls. Is the rat with you?" she asks as she looks over at Rocky at the window.

"Rat? Very funny. I happen to be a rabbit," he says.

"Okay ... Gabrielle, your new look is nice, although I rather liked the way you looked before. What happened to make you change so drastically?" Mrs. Bartell asks.

"Well, that's kind of why we came to talk to you," I reply. "There's something we need to tell you—but first, you might want to sit down."

She looks at Carmen, who nods in agreement. Carmen walks over to the door of the library and closes it so that we won't be overheard. Mrs. Bartell pulls out a chair and is ready to listen.

"I met a witch who said she could help me ..."

I tell Mrs. Bartell the whole story. The more I talk, the

more I realize I am to blame for all of this. When I'm done telling her what happened, she looks at me with fear and worry.

"Gabrielle, this is really bad. It's one thing to make a deal with a witch, but Lady Lydia? She's the worst of the worst," Mrs. Bartell says in a small, sad voice.

"What can you tell us about Lady Lydia?" I ask.

"She's a powerful witch with one goal: to turn Brooklyn into an abyss of white and gray; a place where every leaf, every snowflake, every grain of sand looks exactly the same. She wants every resident of Brooklyn to look, speak, and behave exactly the same—mindlessly.

"To make this happen, Lady Lydia needed to find a kid who just arrived in Brooklyn from a different country. She fed on that kid's culture, customs, and courage. She called it their essence. She needed to collect the essence of one kid from every country. She has collected essences from all but one place—Haiti."

"Why hasn't she been able to get the essence of a Haitian kid?" I ask.

"Because Madam Monday—a good witch—stopped her."

"How?" Carmen says.

"Madam Monday lured her to a graveyard. She used a powerful spell and was able to trap Lady Lydia there. It seems she's managed to break out of the graveyard. And now she's trying to finish what she started. She's trying to collect the essence of a kid from the last country on her list—Haiti. Once she has it, Brooklyn as we all know it will be lost forever."

"Can she just take a kid's essence like that?" Carmen asks.

"A person's essence—their culture, customs, and courage—can't be taken. It has to be given freely," Mrs. Bartell explains.

"So that's why she gave me three wishes," I say. "She needed me to turn away from my culture three times. And once that happens, she will have what she needs to take over all of Brooklyn."

"Exactly. Once she has your essence, it's all over."

"Where's the witch who defeated her before—Madam Monday?" I ask. "Maybe if we find her, she can tell us how to defeat Lady Lydia."

Mrs. Bartell says, "That's just it—no one knows where Madam Monday lives. She hasn't revealed her location in years. Many think that she's a myth. But that's what they thought of Lady Lydia too. And if Lydia is real, then . . ."

"Then so is Madam Monday," I finish.

"Yes, but how do we find her?" Mrs. Bartell wonders out loud.

"I know!" Carmen says. "Mrs. Bartell, Gabrielle, follow me!"

Mrs. Bartell and I look at each other and shrug. I tell Rocky to go recheck my apartment on the off chance that my family's back. He knows it's pointless, but he goes anyway, just to make me feel better. We then follow Carmen down the hallway. She looks in on the classrooms.

"What are you looking for?" I ask.

"What classroom is detention in today?" Carmen asks Mrs. Bartell.

"Just up ahead," she replies. Carmen marches forward.

"Why are we going to detention?" I ask.

"Because that's where we'll find him," Carmen says.

"Find who?" Mrs. Bartell asks.

"The one guy who knows how to get anything for anyone," Carmen says.

Mrs. Bartell and I say his name at the same time: "Getz!"

"Yes! He can get Madam Monday for us," Carmen says.

"Wait, can he? I mean, I know he can get anything, but can he actually get the location of a long-lost witch?" I ask Mrs. Bartell.

Mrs. Bartell thinks it over and says, "Well, he did manage to get me a scarce *Star Trek* action figure that was discontinued."

Carmen says, "A *Star Trek* doll. Oh, for your kids?"

"No, not a doll. Action figure. And no, not for my kids. For me. I'm a Trekkie," Mrs. Bartell proudly says. We all look at her strangely but wisely decide not to say anything.

"Hey, I found him," I announce. Carmen was right: Getz is in detention. Looking bored and ready to leave. We signal to him in the window. He perks up and sneaks out of class.

"Gabrielle. Carmen . . . Trekkie," he says, flashing a smile at Mrs. Bartell.

Mrs. Bartell blushes and turns away.

"What can I do for you ladies?" he says.

"We need you to get us something that no one has seen in forever," I reply.

"And what would that be?"

I take a deep breath and begin, "We're looking for a witch. I know it sounds crazy—"

"What kind of witch?"

"Excuse me?" Carmen says.

"Come on, ladies, be specific. Is this an elemental witch, a sea witch, or a traditional witch?"

"Traditional," I reply.

Getz nods slowly. "Now we're getting somewhere. What's this witch's name?"

"Madam Monday," we all say at once.

"I see . . ." he whispers to himself.

"You know how to find her?" Mrs. Bartell asks.

"Maybe . . . maybe not," Getz says. "That all depends."

"On what?" I ask.

Getz turns his attention to Mrs. Bartell. "That quiz you plan to give us next week?"

"What about it?" she replies suspiciously.

"I have some associates who would prefer the test disappear," Getz says.

"No," she replies.

"All right, perhaps we make it a take-home test?"

"Nope," she replies as they stare each other down.

"I'm not an unreasonable guy—an open-book test," Getz says.

"Can't do it," Mrs. Bartell says.

"Extra five days to study?"

"One day."

"Four days."

"Two."

"Deal." They shake on it.

"Now, take us to Madam Monday," I tell him.

"That's not how this works. I have to make moves. Reach out to a few people. Hit the streets. I'll get back to you in the morning."

"Getz, can you find a family that's gone missing?" I ask.

"Was the family taken by a witch?" he asks.

"Yes."

"Sorry. I can get a witch, but I can't get the things, places, and people they conceal with magic."

"Okay, then please get us Madam Monday. She is our only chance to save my family," I say.

"I'll get started right now," Getz says.

"You're in detention. How are you going to get out of school?" Carmen asks.

He scoffs. "Please. I've got three escape plans for this hall-way alone. Detention . . . you ladies kill me." Getz disappears down the hallway.

"Don't worry, Gabrielle—Getz will find Madam Monday, and she'll show us how to defeat Lady Lydia," Carmen says.

"Yes, but what if she hurts my family in the meantime?" I ask.

Mrs. Bartell puts her hand on my shoulder and says, "Lady Lydia knows how important your family is to you. She's going to keep them safe and use them as a bargaining chip. She won't hurt them—at least not right now. Tomorrow we will start fresh and work with the good witch. Until then, go home and try to get some rest. You're gonna need it."

———

Rocky did not find anyone at my place. I knew he wouldn't. He then went to the park to see if anyone knew anything. I would have stopped him, but I think he wanted to feel like he was helping. Carmen would not let me go home and be alone. She insisted I have dinner at her house.

"Are you sure?" I ask.

"Yes, you are coming with me," she says as we leave my building.

I have never been to Carmen's house, and I'm not sure what to expect. I'm grateful that she invited me to dinner, but I'm not sure I'm a good guest to have right now. I'm so worried about my family that I can't think of anything else.

"Gabrielle, when we get inside, you have to promise me something," Carmen says just before she opens the door.

"What is it?"

"Promise that you will try to relax—just for dinner. We are going to get your family back. But for now, I know your aunt and uncle wouldn't want you sad the whole night. So tonight, try to have a good time, and tomorrow we will deal with the witch. Okay?"

I'm not sure I can relax, not with everything going on. But she has been so good to me, the least I can do is try.

"Okay, worrying is not allowed tonight."

"Good—and before we go in, I should warn you, my house is like a circus right now," she says.

"Why? What's happening?"

"It's my sister Gloria's quinceañera in a few days."

"What's that?" I ask.

"Gloria is turning fifteen. In Mexico, we celebrate the fifteenth birthday with a big party, to mark the passage from girlhood to womanhood. Although I'm not really sure I'd call Gloria a woman yet. This morning she knocked our little brother down trying to get the last of the Fruity Pebbles cereal."

I laugh, she opens the door, and we walk in together.

Carmen's place is decorated with family pictures and large candles in glass tubes with images of saints. The house is full of activity. I count seven people in the living room alone. They move in different directions, speaking both English and Spanish. At the center of all the attention is Carmen's sister Gloria. She's wearing a big, beautiful white ball gown with purple flowers. It cascades down to the floor. She looks like she belongs on a bright, glamorous wedding cake.

"They've tried on the dress a hundred times, but Gloria and my mom wanted to try it on again. Just to be sure," Carmen says.

"It's a really big thing in Mexico, huh?" I reply as I gaze at Gloria's dress.

"Yeah, my family has been preparing for it for over a year.

We have a bunch of people coming: aunts, uncles, cousins, and their cousins. It's going to be in a big church, and the reception is in a really big dance hall."

"There's going to be a dance?" I ask.

The woman adjusting Gloria's dress laughs. "A dance? No! There will be many, many dances!"

"Mom, this is my friend from school, Gabrielle," Carmen says.

Mrs. Hernández is short, with a round face, dark eyes, and dark hair. She has the same kind eyes that Carmen has. And when she smiles, the house lights up. She shouts something to the crowd, and they all yell back, "*Hola, Gabrielle!*"

"*Hola!*" I reply. I turn to Carmen's mom. "Thank you for inviting me to dinner, Mrs. Hernández. I don't know what you're making, but it smells delicious."

"You can call me Mrs. H, okay? I'm making Carmen's favorite: posole. It's a hearty soup with chicken, chili peppers, and my secret seasoning. We also have tamales. It's a typical traditional Mexican meal. What are some traditional Haitian meals, Gabrielle?"

I'm excited to tell her about the meals my mom makes in Haiti. There are so many that I love that I don't know where to start. "Well, my mom makes . . . There's a dish called . . . um . . . I love when she cooks . . ."

I can't remember. Oh no! I can't remember one meal my mom has made. And the harder I try, the more nothing comes to mind. What's going on?

I look at Carmen, panic in my eyes. She comes to my rescue.

"Gabrielle is thirsty, Mom. I'm gonna get her something to drink," Carmen says as she takes my hand and guides me to the kitchen.

"What happened? Why couldn't you answer?" Carmen asks.

"I tried to, but nothing came out," I reply. "When I think about the foods I love back in Haiti, I just see a blank space."

"You think the witch—"

Before Carmen can finish her question, one of her relatives enters the kitchen. She smiles as she checks on the food and adds water to one of many pots on the stove.

We can't talk like we want to because every few seconds, someone comes into the kitchen. I lean over and whisper to Carmen, "I think Lady Lydia took more than just my family. All my memories of family dinners in Haiti are gone."

"I'm sorry."

"It's okay." It's not okay. It's like with every passing minute, I'm losing another part of me.

Carmen's dad enters the kitchen and says something in Spanish. Carmen tells me that he invited me to come to the backyard, where they are practicing a special dance for the ceremony.

"Yes, in a quinceañera, there are a few dances. And one of the most important ones is the father-daughter dance. And someday, I will have that dance with my Carmen," her dad says in English as he pinches her cheeks.

"Dad, company," Carmen reminds him. Her cheeks glow red with embarrassment. But that doesn't stop Mr. H from squeezing her other cheek.

"I'm sorry, *mi hija,* I can't help it. Your quinceañera will be the last one this family has."

He gets weepy and takes a tissue out of his pocket to wipe his eyes.

"Oh no! Carlos, no more tears. Go and get ready to rehearse the dance," Mrs. H says as she enters the kitchen. Mr. H nods and walks out.

Mrs. H shakes her head. "I thought I was the emotional one, but my husband . . . he might flood the church with his happy tears."

"Mom, he pinched my cheeks. We had a deal," Carmen says.

"I know, I know. Not in front of company. But he can't help it. He loves you. That's what dads do. And moms . . . we worry. Gabrielle, I'm happy you're here with us, but I'm sorry that things are so crazy in the house tonight."

"That's okay. I like crazy," I reply.

"Good, then you are in the right place. Have you ever been to a quinceañera before?"

"No, Mrs. H, I haven't."

"Well, you are invited to this one. We would love to have you."

"Thank you. I'll ask my aunt and uncle."

Well, that is, if they are still alive.

"Tell me, what are some of the events you celebrate in Haiti?" she asks.

"Um, a lot. We celebrate . . ."

My mind goes blank. I can't recall one celebration in ten years of being alive. How is that possible?

"Gabrielle? Are you okay?" Carmen's mom asks.

"Huh? Yeah, I'm fine."

Carmen tries to rescue me again. "Gabrielle's parents are still in Haiti, Mom, and I think—"

"Oh, don't tell me. It's hard to talk about back home because it makes you miss it, right?"

"Yeah, something like that," I mumble.

"I understand. It's not easy being an immigrant. Sometimes you get so homesick. The day I came to this country, it happened to be Mexican Independence Day. It's one of the most sacred days in Mexico. It's on September sixteenth. And in Mexico, there are fireworks, dancing, and lots of food. I was so sad to miss it. When is Haiti's independence day?"

"I . . . can't remember," I admit.

"Oh . . . okay. My husband collects coffee mugs with flags on them. And now that we know a Haitian family, we'll get a flag of Haiti to add to the collection."

"That sounds nice, Mrs. H."

"What colors are the Haitian flag?"

"They are . . . um . . ."

Oh no, not the flag too!

"Mom, let's go to the rehearsal before Dad gets weepy again," Carmen says.

"Yes, you're right. Oh, and Gabrielle, you can have some tamales to tide you over until dinner."

"Can I have some too?" Carmen says.

"Okay, but just one!" Mrs. H says as she heads out of the kitchen.

"Thanks for the rescue," I say. "I can't believe I don't even know the colors of my flag."

"We can look it up later," Carmen replies. But remember, you promised to try to have a good time, right?"

"Yeah, you're right."

Carmen takes the lids off the pots on the stove, and the delicious scent hits my nose and reminds me that I'm hungry.

"This pot has chicken tamales, and the other pot has pork. And this last pot has sweet tamales, flavored with pineapples. Pick whichever one you like," she says. I take a chicken, and she takes the sweet one with fruit. We head out to the back of her building for dance rehearsal.

I watch Carmen and her family as they do a dance routine. The boys have their movements, and the girls have theirs. Then they join in and dance together. They even let me dance with them. I mess up a lot, but that's okay, because it's fun.

When we're done, we go inside for dinner. There are so many different dishes on the table, not just the soup and the tamales. The dinner is so good that I eat until my stomach almost pops.

I look around. I love the heat rising off the homemade tortillas, the amazing scent of the soup, and the laughter around the table. This isn't Carmen's house. It's her home. I had a home. And I gave that away.

CHAPTER FOURTEEN
Be a Tomato

CARMEN'S FAMILY INVITES ME to spend the night. I pretend to call my family and ask them if I can stay. I hate lying, but it's better this way. When it's time to get ready for bed, Carmen lets me wear her favorite Alvin and the Chipmunks pajamas. Her mom goes around to everyone's bedroom and kisses them good night on the forehead. She kisses me too so I won't feel left out. Carmen says she hates it, but I think she kind of likes it.

I'm so tired that I could sleep for a whole year, but when I close my eyes, sleep doesn't come to me. I'm too busy worrying about my family. Did the witch throw them inside a volcano, into a boiling sea of lava? Could they be roaming the frozen tundra, one icy breath away from death? Or did the witch throw them into a den of hungry lions, thirsty for blood?

It's no use trying to sleep. I walk over to the other side of the bedroom, where Carmen is sleeping. Her hair is all over the place, she's kicked the covers off, and she's scowling and talking in her sleep.

"Bow to the laser tag master!" she says.

"You tell 'em, Carmen!" I say as I cover her back up. I walk around the apartment softly, careful not to wake anyone. I need to go get some air and think about how I can make it up to my family when I get them back.

If I get them back.

Carmen left me out some clothes to go to school with in the morning, so I change into them and quietly step out for a walk. Summer just started, but I can tell it's going to be my favorite season. My family talked about going to the beach for the summer and staying by the water for the whole day. We also talked about going to the summer street fair in downtown Brooklyn as soon as school let out. I guess none of that will happen now.

Gabrielle, stop thinking like that. You will find your family.

I sigh loudly and walk past the storefronts. Carmen's neighborhood is like mine: there are a lot of corner stores, liquor stores, and meat markets. I walk past the laundromat, coffee shop, and a church. I'm not sure where I'm going, but I keep walking. Some small part of me thinks that maybe I'll walk past one of the storefronts and see my aunt and uncle inside.

Yeah, I know. Crazy.

"And what do you think you're doing, young lady!" an old man says as he comes out of the meat market. It's Mr. Jung.

He owns the butcher shop on my block. He has a potbelly and thin mustache, and his glasses are always crooked. He knows my aunt very well. She comes to him to buy her meats, and sometimes, if he gets a meat delivery he thinks my aunt will like, he sets it aside for her.

"Hi, Mr. Jung. What are you doing here?" I ask.

"I own this store and the butcher shop in your neighborhood. Now I have a question: Where are you going at this time of night, and why isn't your aunt with you?"

"I'm sleeping over at a friend's house. I just came out to get some air. I'll go back in a minute," I reply.

"This is your first summer in Brooklyn, huh? Well, it's going to get a lot hotter, just you wait."

"Yeah," I mumble with my head down.

He looks at me closely. "Gabrielle, is everything okay?"

"Can I ask you something?"

"Sure, come inside. I'll get you a cold drink to cool down before you go back to your friend's house," he says. I follow him into the meat market. He hands me a cold soda and invites me to sit on a crate near the cash register.

"I didn't know people go food shopping late at night," I admit.

"Oh yeah, many people only shop at night. There are fewer lines, less hassle. And many of my customers are working moms. They don't have time to make it down here until after closing. So I try to keep the market open later. Now, what was it you wanted to ask me?"

"Where are you from?"

"My family was born in South Korea."

"Was it hard to be here because you're not American?"

"What do you mean, Gabrielle? Of course I'm an American."

"You are?" I ask, not sure I heard him right.

"Why yes, I am."

"Can you be American and not be from here?"

"Of course you can."

"I don't understand," I admit.

"Look around this market. It's a good representation of what it means to be an American. There are shoppers from all different backgrounds. There's Mrs. Ferrari in aisle three. She's from Italy, and she's a schoolteacher." I follow his gaze to see a beanpole-thin woman with a grocery basket in her hand.

"And over there in aisle five are Mr. and Mrs. Oni; they're here from Nigeria. And that older lady over there, in aisle one, is Ms. Tsosie. She's Native American. Her people called this land home long before anyone else." He watches Ms. Tsosie closely as she feels her way through a stack of produce. "Ms. Tsosie, go easy on that avocado."

"I have to feel it, make sure it's right for me," Ms. Tsosie shouts back.

"It's not your boyfriend; it's a fruit."

She rolls her eyes and picks up another avocado.

"The point is this, Gabrielle: America is made up of immigrants. Immigrants like you and me. This country is strong because of its many different cultures and backgrounds."

"So being an immigrant is a good thing?"

"Oh yes, it's a very good thing."

"But what if I want to be an American?"

"Why can't you be both Haitian and American? Come take a look at this," he says as he walks over to a bin full of tomatoes.

He holds one in his hand and shows it to me. "These beautiful tomatoes are both a vegetable and fruit at the same time. They don't worry about being one or the other. The great thing about this country is that we do not have to either. Be the tomato. Be Haitian. Be American."

"I never thought about being both," I reply.

"Well, think about it. It's important to be proud of your past as well as your future—that's it! Ms. Tsosie, put down the avocado!" he says, rushing over to Ms. Tsosie.

"What did I do?" she asks.

"You squeezed it so hard, it's guacamole now!" he replies. The two of them start to argue about the right amount of pressure to apply to fruit. Then someone calls my name.

"Gabrielle!"

I look over and see an older lady waving to me. It's Mrs. Anderson, my aunt's Jamaican friend. She's the one who wanted me to have dinner with her and her granddaughter. She has a basket in her hand full of meats, veggies, and Caribbean spices.

"Hi, Mrs. Anderson," I say.

"Hello, sweetheart! Where's your aunt?" she asks, scanning the store.

"Ah, she's around somewhere," I reply.

"She didn't show up on the bus today. Is everything okay?"

"Um . . . yeah. She had some stuff she had to do, but she's fine."

"Oh, okay. I didn't know she shopped at night as I do. It's just better. There are no long lines, no big crowds. It's the best."

"That's what I hear."

"Have you seen Mr. Jung? I need more Scotch bonnet peppers. The bin is empty," she says.

"I think he's over there with Ms. Tsosie," I say, pointing toward them.

She looks over and says, "She's molesting the avocados again."

"Yeah, I think so."

"Never mind that. We were supposed to have you over to dinner. When can we do that?"

"Not sure. Things have been crazy around the house. I will have my aunt call you."

"That sounds good, but since you're here now, you should meet my angel—my granddaughter. I know she's here somewhere . . ." Mrs. Anderson looks around for a few moments.

I'm not really in the mood to meet new people. Also, I have too much on my mind to worry about making new friends. But I don't say anything because I don't want to hurt her feelings. She looks around a little more but can't seem to locate her granddaughter.

"Maybe I can meet her another time—" I start.

"Wait! She's right over there!" Mrs. Anderson says. I look down and my sneakers are untied. I bend down to tie them; when I come back up, I come face to face with Mrs. Anderson's granddaughter—Tianna.

What the heck?

"This is my angel," Mrs. Anderson says proudly.

Our eyes meet, and all of Brooklyn stands still. It's like we're the only two around. Her eyes are wide with shock and alarm. My mouth is open, and I can't remember how to close it. My heart is racing, and I feel like someone poured a bucket of ice water on me.

"You two look like you've seen a ghost or something. Do you know each other from school?"

We don't answer Mrs. Anderson right away. We can't. The shock is just too much to take in, and we need a few more seconds—or maybe a full year. Wow. Just wow.

"Gabrielle, do you know my angel?" Mrs. Anderson asks again.

Oh yeah, I know your demon granddaughter. She's awful! She's mean, she's cruel, and I can't stand her. She's the reason my life has been hell since I got here. I wish she went to another school—no, I don't want to have any other kid feel the way Tianna made me feel. I wish she were on another planet. Yes, that's it!

Mrs. Anderson, your angel brings nothing but hell to everyone she meets. Pack her stuff and ship her off this planet, so we never have to see her mean, spiteful face again!

"Gabrielle, have you met my angel before?"

I look at Tianna. The shock has almost worn off, and what

remains is fear. She's afraid that I'm going to tell her grandmother the truth. Her eyes are pleading with me. I want the truth to come out. I want everyone to know how awful Tianna is. Then I look at Mrs. Anderson's face.

"No, Mrs. Anderson, I don't know your angel. Hi, Tianna. I'm Gabrielle."

She swallows hard, and I can almost feel the relief sinking into her body.

"Well, you two get to know each other. I need to go over to the meat section; I'm making goat head stew, and I almost forgot the goat head!" Mrs. Anderson laughs.

"Goat head?" I ask, never taking my eyes off Tianna.

"Yes, goat head stew. It's my great-grandmother's recipe. And it's Tianna's favorite."

"Really? That's so good to know," I reply as I stare her down. Tianna looks off to the side. Her grandmother walks away to get the meat, leaving her "angel" and me to talk alone.

"Why didn't you tell her we knew each other?" she asks as soon as her grandmother is out of earshot.

"I was planning to, but then . . ."

"Then what?"

"Then I saw the look on her face. Your grandmother is proud of you. She loves you—like, a lot. I didn't want to make her sad and tell her the truth—that her grandchild is a nightmare."

"Yeah, but now you're gonna go to school and tell everyone you saw me at the market with a goat head and a basket full of crazy island seasoning. You'll tell them all about my grandmother and her colorful outfits that don't match what other grownups are wearing. And they will make fun of me. Fine! I don't care."

She's lying. I can tell by the way she can't look at me. I can also tell by the tears that spring up in her eyes. "You care, Tianna. You care—a lot."

"Okay, okay, fine! You win! What do I have to do to get you not to tell everyone?"

"Were you born in Jamaica?" I ask.

"Yes."

"Do you ever go back there?" I ask.

She angrily chews on her lower lip. "I go every year."

"Then why do you make fun of me? You're from a small island, just like me."

"I don't know. I just . . . It's what they do here," she mumbles.

"No, it's what *you* do. And you didn't have to. You made me feel so . . ." I can't finish my thought. I'm not going to cry at a meat market.

"I made you feel what?" she asks.

"Forget it," I reply, shaking my head.

"Say it—"

"Small! Okay? You made me feel . . . like I didn't matter. But now I see you. I see the real you."

"What does that mean?" she demands.

"It means I was wrong to let your words get to me. I'm done with that now. You can call me whatever you want. You can make fun of me. But I know whatever you say to me, you are really saying it to yourself. We're the same. Different island, but still the same thing."

"If you don't tell anyone, then I'll stop teasing you. I'll be your friend."

I shake my head sadly. "I have friends—real ones. Ones who tell me that I'm okay just the way I am. And that I don't need to change. Maybe you should get some friends like that," I inform her. I turn to walk away, and she stops me.

"Are you going to tell everyone at school you saw me here?" she asks, terrified.

"You're making the same mistake I made. You're hiding who you are because you think it will make people like you. But that doesn't work. And what's the point of them liking you if it's not really you?"

"So you're going to tell them you saw me?" she says, sounding defeated and sad.

I look at her and how scared she is. I was scared too—scared to be the new Haitian girl. Afraid to be me. And it cost me everything.

"Don't worry, Tianna. I didn't see you here tonight."

"Really?" she says in disbelief.

"Yeah, but you should know that until you tell the truth about who you are and where you're from, no one sees the real you."

CHAPTER FIFTEEN
FEAR

THE NEXT MORNING, we meet up with Rocky in front of Carmen's building. We offer to take him on the bus with us so we can all meet Getz together. But Rocky says he'll join us later; he has a yoga class he can't miss.

"Yoga?" Carmen asks.

"Yeah, it helps keep me centered," Rocky says casually. Carmen and I look at each other and decide it's best just to nod along.

When the bus comes, we take our seats, and the kids on the bus are friendlier to me. Kim—the girl who didn't invite me to her party—now wants me to sit with her at lunch. She says she's sorry for not inviting me and that she can't remember why she didn't. It's possible the witch made her forget that I'm Haitian.

Kim is not the only one who forgets I wasn't born here. The other kids talk about movies and TV shows that I don't know about because I was in Haiti at the time. But when I tell them that, they laugh and tell me to stop being silly. According to them, I was in the same preschool classes they were. Well, that's one thing we can say about Lady Lydia: when she grants a wish, she goes all out.

When we get to school, most of the staff is busy getting ready for Culture Day. It's scheduled for tomorrow in the auditorium. The hallways are covered with flags from all over the world. The desks and chairs in some of the classrooms have been rearranged to make room for long tables that display games from other countries.

There's also a sign-up sheet for kids who want to talk about where they are from. You put your name in one column, and in the other column, you put the country you are from. I go over to that table to sign up, but when I put the country I'm from, the ink disappears. I show it to Carmen.

"It won't even let you write the word *Haiti?*" she says.

"No," I say.

"Try again," she says.

I lean down on the table and write *Haiti* in small, neat letters. Nothing happens. The ink remains. Carmen and I smile at each other, but then seconds later, the ink disappears yet again.

"Argh!"

"It's okay. Let's go get Mrs. Bartell, and the three of us can find Getz."

And as we walk down the bustling hallway, I tell Carmen about meeting Tianna. She can't believe it.

"But don't tell anyone, I told her I would not share her secret," I add.

"I won't, but why are you being so nice to her? She wasn't that nice to you," Carmen says.

"Yeah, but I did bad stuff too. I hit her, and I shouldn't have done that. I lied to my family about where my perfect English came from, I got you in trouble, and I caused my entire family to disappear."

"Everyone makes mistakes," Carmen says.

"Yeah, that's what my dad says." As soon as I bring him up, I feel pain in my stomach. I miss my parents so much.

"Do you think Tianna will be nicer to you now?"

"I don't know what she'll do. But I know what I'll do if I ever get my family back—be honest and be myself. I love Haiti. And now I can't remember anything about it. Carmen, it was my homeland. And I don't care if that sign-up sheet won't let me put down Haiti—tomorrow I'm going to speak at Culture Day."

"Are you sure?"

"Yeah, I never want to forget where I came from—not again," I reply as we enter the library. It's even more chaotic in there than it is in the school hallways. Mrs. Bartell is telling the students what books go where and showing them how to decorate the room. It already looks pretty amazing. There are books displayed by famous writers from around the world. She sees us and quickly comes over. She seems a little ... frazzled.

"Mrs. Bartell, are you all right?" I ask.

"We ordered a dozen books on the country of Turkey, and they sent us a dozen books about raising and caring for turkeys—as in the animals!" she replies. "The people who are supposed to set up the lights and sound in the auditorium are late; the flag that was supposed to represent Peru is actually Canada's flag. And the cassette tape we were planning on playing over the speakers was supposed to have national anthems from the entire world—instead, it has six hours of yodeling."

I touch her arm, and Carmen does too. Mrs. Bartell looks at us and shakes her head.

"I'm sorry. I know you girls have a lot more important things on your mind. Getz has something for you two; he's waiting in the yard. I wish I could go along, but I'm afraid I can't get away right now."

"It's okay. You take care of Culture Day, and we'll find the good witch," Carmen says.

"If you need anything, just ask. And do not do anything dangerous or crazy."

"We'll try not to," I reply. Mrs. Bartell writes us a note in case a teacher stops us. She moves to hand us the note, but she's hesitating.

"What is it, Mrs. Bartell?" Carmen says.

"I should leave this stuff and go with you two. Getting Gabrielle's family back is important."

"Yeah, but so is Culture Day," I say. "Stay here and help make sure it goes well. Oh, and the witch did something to the sign-up sheet; it won't let me put Haiti on the list. Do you think you can do it for me?"

"You want to make a presentation?" Mrs. Bartell asks.

"Yes, it's the least I can do after everything," I reply.

"But wait, how can you do a presentation when you can't remember anything about Haiti?" Carmen says.

"All I know is that I owe it to Haiti to try," I say.

"All right, I'll sign you up, Gabrielle," Mrs. Bartell says.

"And Rocky should be here soon. When you see him, send him our way," Carmen says.

"Okay, I will. Good luck, girls," Mrs. Bartell says as we rush out of the room.

———

We get outside just in time to see Rocky racing across the street. We call him over, and together we head over to Getz. He's leaning on a pole with his customary trench coat and hat. He scans the yard and makes sure that there are no kids near us.

"Ladies," he says. He then looks down at Rocky. "Rocky."

"How did you know his name?" Carmen asks.

"Rocky and I have done business before. He was looking for the perfect rabbit ears. I made some calls. Didn't I?" Getz says.

"Yeah . . . thanks," Rocky says, suddenly uneasy.

"You don't call me anymore to get you rabbit ears to try on; does that mean you found another way to become a rabbit?"

"I . . . took care of it," Rocky says.

Getz turns to us. "All right, I have good news and bad news."

"Well, what happened—did you find Madam Monday?" I ask.

"I had to call in a lot of favors and search all of Brooklyn to get a lead. But when I finally did, it led me to a warlock down on Flatbush Ave. He's retired, so he didn't know much, but he pointed me to a witch friend of his who worked downtown. She pointed me to a powerful witch who lived on the edge of town. Figured I'd check out the place in case she was still there."

"And did you find her?" Carmen asks.

"No, she was gone, moved out. I got in touch with the neighbor, and according to her, the witch is still in Brooklyn, but she has no idea where. So, I used all my resources, and it took all night, but I finally found her."

"Where?" Rocky asks.

"Where most witches hang out—Subway."

"The train?" I ask.

"The restaurant. I forgot how much witches love cold cuts."

"Okay, so did you get her?" Rocky asks.

"That's the bad news—she was already gone. But on her way out, she dropped an earring. And now this is the only clue we have to go by," Getz says as he takes out an earring from his pocket and hands it to me.

"How are we going to find her with just an earring?" Carmen asks.

I look it over and grin wildly. "We need candy," I announce.

"Gabrielle, I'm all for a sugar rush, but shouldn't we focus on getting your family back?" Carmen asks.

"No, you don't get it. The earring. What are these?" I ask her.

Carmen looks at the colorful earring and says, "Parakeets."

"Yeah, and where was the last time we saw earrings with colorful parakeets?"

"The candy lady!" she shouts excitedly. Some of the kids in the yard turn to us to see what's happening. We smile awkwardly and act like nothing is going on. When they go back to their games, we go back to business.

"You really think the candy lady is Madam Monday?" Getz asks.

"Only one way to find out," Rocky says, as he takes off across the street.

"Thanks, Getz," I shout as Carmen and I follow Rocky to the candy lady's window.

We bang on the window and wait for her to open it. When nothing happens, we bang again, but this time louder. She opens the window and looks down at us.

"You know the rules: I only sell candy at recess. Come back in a few hours," she says, closing the window in our faces.

"Let's try her door. That way she'll know we're not here for candy," Carmen suggests. So, we all go around to the front door. It's bright red and has wildflowers on it. We knock, and she opens and sees that once again it's us.

"You kids are pests! No sugar this early in the morning,

and you keep going like this and you will be on my 'no sale' list!" she says as she goes to close the door on us.

"Madam Monday!" I shout as the door closes. We wait to see if she'll open the door again. Nothing. Carmen and I look at each other sadly. This is the only lead we have. Now what? Just when we are about to leave, the bright red door opens back up again.

"This isn't about candy, is it?" the candy lady asks.

"No. It's about my family," I reply.

"What about them?"

"They're gone. And we need your help," Carmen says.

"Who took them?" the candy lady asks.

I reply, "Lady Lydia."

And right away, her face changes. Her eyes grow dark with concern. Her posture stiffens, and her eyes dart back and forth.

"You'd better come in," she says.

We enter her apartment, and we're not ready for what we find in there—a room full of doors.

"Each one leads to a different part of the world. How do you think I'm able to bring you candy from anywhere?" she asks.

We all look at each other but don't say anything. She invites us to sit down on her cloud-shaped sofa. Yes, it's literally shaped like a cloud.

"Now, how do you know about Lady Lydia? Have you been messing around in the graveyard? Is that what this is about?

Did all of you kids dare each other to go inside the graveyard? Speak!" she demands.

"We didn't," I say.

"Gabrielle is right. We never went anywhere near a graveyard. Lady Lydia came to her," Carmen says.

"No! That's not possible. She's imprisoned," the candy lady says. We all look at her; she reads the expressions on our faces and begins to whisper something. Then she waves her hand in front of her face, and a small portal opens in the middle of the air, showing us an abandoned graveyard. She searches through the portal.

"I can't feel her energy. She's not in the graveyard," the candy lady says.

"That's what we wanted to tell you," I say. "She's escaped. She offered to give me three wishes in exchange for my essence."

"You're from Haiti. The final place she needs to collect."

"Yes, and does this mean you're Madam Monday?" Carmen asks.

"Yes, I am. This is all my fault. I should have ended Lydia when I had the chance. But it's so hard to end things with a friend."

"You and the bad witch were once on the same side?" I ask.

"Yes, we were."

"What happened?" Carmen asks.

"We were chosen to care for this area," Madam Monday begins. "Brooklyn was ours to look after and to protect.

Everyday people from different parts of the world would settle here. There were times when one group didn't get along with the other. That would cause strife and tension among the community. And that's where Lydia came in.

"She worked hard to find a solution to the disharmony in the neighborhood. I told her that it was only a matter of time and that things would settle down. And they did, but for Lydia, it was too much to wait. She didn't want any arguing or discord at all.

"She came up with an idea—why not make all the humans the same? That way, no one would ever argue or get into fights. There would be nothing to disagree on if everyone was the same.

"In her mind, she was giving the world a gift—the gift of assimilation. That means everyone would act the exact same way. Like a copy of each other."

"She was obsessed with what she called 'perfection,' which meant that everything and everyone is to be the same.

"And to make sure no one got in her way, she created an army. She took the most dangerous parts of various animals and put them together. She created creatures with venom, claws, and wings and allowed them to be invisible until she wanted them to be seen. She called them the Flying Evil Army of Rage; FEAR. And they had only one mission: do Lydia's bidding."

"Did they do her bidding?" Rocky asks.

"Oh yes! She was able to use them to scare the kids, and adults, too. I finally had to step in and stop her. I couldn't do away with her completely, or maybe I didn't want to, since we were friends at one point. Anyway, she's back now, and this time, Gabrielle, you have to do the one thing I couldn't —you have put an end to Lydia, once and for all. Now tell me you didn't make a wish yet." Her eyes are looking right through me.

"I made two of them," I confess as I lower my head.

"You made two wishes?" she yells. The cloud we're sitting on starts to shake and sputter. It throws us off and down to the floor.

"Sorry. I didn't mean to get so upset. Oscar is connected to my emotions. If I'm upset, he's upset," she says as she looks at the sofa.

"You named your sofa Oscar?" Rocky asks.

"Of course. Oscar's a good name for a cloud. Now, Gabrielle, why in the name of all that is good would you make two wishes?"

I quickly tell her the story, and she listens carefully.

"And now, my family is gone. What do I do?" I ask.

"This is some pickle you've gotten yourself into. But if I had made the spell stronger, it would have kept Lady Lydia in place. Well, no, because sooner or later, she would have gotten free. Well, that doesn't mean we're not to blame . . ." Madam Monday is having a conversation with herself. She starts to argue back and forth about whether it was her fault or not.

"Um, excuse me. Can we get back to my missing family?" I ask.

"Oh, yes. Sorry. I just hate that I wasn't able to keep her locked up for good," Madam Monday says.

"But you can fix that now, can't you? You can lock her back up or something? Maybe drop a house on her like in *The Wizard of Oz*?" Carmen asks.

"It's not that simple, Carmen," Madam Monday says.

"Why not?" Rocky asks as he pokes the cloud sofa.

"Lady Lydia is a very clever witch. She knows that I can't interfere with a deal that has taken place in good faith. Now, did she hurt you and force you to make a deal with her?"

"No, I guess not," I reply.

"Did she make you eat or drink anything that played with your mind to make you say yes to the deal?"

"No, Madam Monday. She didn't," I reply.

"Then it was a fair deal, and there's nothing I can do to stop it. And she's too powerful now. I won't be able to put her back into the graveyard."

"There has to be a way to get her to return my family. And set the kids in the stream free," I say.

"Lady Lydia has gotten strong thanks to all the essences she's collected from all the kids. If you set them free, that should diminish her powers. And when that happens, all the magic she's done should come undone," Madam Monday tells us.

"Then maybe I can get my family back?"

"Exactly," Madam Monday replies.

"Okay, so how do we set the kids free?" I ask.

"The stream has a thin layer on top that keeps all the essences trapped. It blocks them from breaking free. There's an animal that feeds on protective coatings just like the one in the stream. It's native to Haiti. It's called the candy cane snail. Before Lydia was trapped in the graveyard, she killed all the snails because she knew they could be used against her. I managed to save one—just one."

"I know it! It has colors on its shell that go around in circles," I say.

"Yes, that's the one you need. But now there is only one left in existence. And to make sure Lydia didn't kill it, I enchanted it so that only the person who has struck a deal with Lydia can hold it. If anyone else tries to hold it with their bare hands, it will sear their skin."

"Where can we find the snail?" I ask.

"You have to go get the snail in the forest just beyond that door," Madam Monday says, motioning toward the door a few feet away from us.

"I just walk through that door and grab a snail?" I ask.

"Yes, but there are traps."

"She can't go alone. Gabrielle needs us to go with her," Rocky says.

"You don't have a choice; only one person through the door at a time," Madam Monday says. "And only the person who made the deal can hold the snail. Otherwise, it will burn you. There's a portal right through there. Be warned: there will be evil things waiting for you on the other side of that door. Are you ready?"

I don't answer. I keep thinking about how powerful Lady Lydia is and how weak I have been. If I weren't weak, I would have never gotten into this mess to begin with, and now look: my family is paying for my mistakes.

"Gabrielle, are you ready to go through that door?" Madam Monday asks.

"It's all my fault. I'm weak; I couldn't resist her offer," I reply.

"Gabrielle, why do you think Lady Lydia picked you?" Madam Monday asks.

"Because I'm from Haiti and she needs my essence to destroy Brooklyn."

"Well, yes, but why you? Other kids from Haiti live in Brooklyn. You're not the only one. So why, out of a hundred kids, did she choose you to be the one to give her your essence? Why you and not someone else?"

I think about it for a moment, but I can't come up with an answer. I shrug, and she smiles warmly.

"Gabrielle, she picked you because you are special. You have courage like no one else I've seen in a long time. That means your essence is stronger than most. And that will give her even more powers. That's why she picked you. But that's also the reason you will defeat her."

"Do you really think I can?" I ask.

"It doesn't matter what I think. I need you to believe that you are strong enough and courageous enough for this battle. Do you believe that?"

I look out the window because I don't want to face Madam

Monday or my friends. The good witch turns me to face her and says, "It seems that along the way, you've forgotten just how special you are. Allow me to remind you . . ." She waves her hand, and I am standing in the middle of my village.

"What am I doing here?" I ask.

"No one can see you. You're inside your own memories. Do you see yourself over there?" she asks.

I follow her gaze and watch a younger version of myself help my mom carry gallons of water from our well into the house.

"You were too little to carry them, but you wanted to help so bad that you found a way to make it work. It took you seven trips, but you did it. You helped your mom get water from the well."

"I remember that. I was so excited to help."

"She knew that you wanted to ease her load, and it made her proud. And take a look over there. Who is that girl who is helping to hide a friend from soldiers who came to do him harm?"

I look where she's pointing, and I see a boy from our village—Jessie—being chased by soldiers. He quickly enters my house, and I hide him under my bed. I had forgotten that.

"I was so afraid that soldiers would hurt him and then hurt us for hiding him," I say.

"Yes, but even though you were afraid, you did everything you could to help out. That's part of who you are. And if you need any more proof of just how brave you can be—look right behind you."

I turn around, and suddenly we are standing on the edge of a cliff. I see the other version of myself jump off the cliff and down to the water below.

"I remember this—Stephanie's mom. She was drowning in grief."

"Yes, and you helped get her back to shore," Madam Monday says. "It's that kind of thing that makes you special. You have to believe in that."

I look over at myself helping Stephanie's mom make it out of the raging waters. I didn't stop to be afraid that day. I didn't worry that I was going to mess things up. I just did what I thought was right. I did that back then, and that's what I will do now—no matter what.

Madam Monday waves her hand, and suddenly we are back inside her house. Carmen says I just disappeared before her eyes. I tell her where I was and what I saw.

"Are you ready to face whatever is on the other side of that door, so you can find the snail and defeat Lydia?" Madam Monday asks.

CHAPTER SIXTEEN
Only Hope

MADAM MONDAY TRIES TO PREPARE ME for what's on the other side of the door. She tells me that there are three obstacles I have to overcome to get to the snail I need.

"Do you know what those obstacles are?" I ask.

"No, I don't. I'm sorry," she replies.

"But Madam Monday, when you saved the last snail, you kept it in a forest for the person who might need it," Carmen says. "Why don't you know the traps that are there? Didn't you set them up?"

"I placed the snail under the protection of the forest. The forest is a living, breathing thing. It makes its own rules. The only thing I know for sure is that you will be tested in three different ways. And you have to be ready, Gabrielle, because if you fail any of the three tests, you won't get to the snail, and your family will never return."

"Okay, I got it," I say.

"Each test is specific to you. You will have ten minutes to

find the snail and bring him out with you. If you can't do it in ten minutes, the door will close, and you will be left inside the forest forever. So be quick, be brave, and, most of all, be clever."

"You can do this, Gabrielle," Carmen says.

"Yup, she's got this!" Rocky adds.

We do a quick group hug, and Madam Monday hands me a silver antique stopwatch. "It's set for ten minutes. Go, quickly! And remember, things may not be what they seem."

She opens the door, there's a blinding light, and I walk through, stopwatch in hand.

———

I step inside and hear the door close behind me. The light dies down, and I find myself in a lush forest with bright green trees that almost touch the sky. The forest is dense, and it's hard to see ahead. I hear someone sobbing. I follow the voice and come to a clearing a few yards away.

"Stephanie!" I call out to my best friend, who's sitting at the base of a tree weeping. "What's wrong? What are you doing here?" I ask as I run over to her.

"You left me," she cries.

"What?"

"You went to America, and you left me. I was your best friend, and you left me behind. How could you? How could you leave me?"

I swallow hard. "Stephanie, I love you so much. Please don't cry."

"You left me and all of our friends, and you went to America. How could you?" As soon as she says that, all my other friends from Haiti appear at the base of the tree. They start chanting together, "How could you leave us? How could you?"

"I didn't want to leave you guys, but I didn't have a choice," I say.

Stephanie says, "That was before. Now you have a choice. You can stay with us. Can you do that, please? Can you stay with us?"

"Well . . . I . . ."

They all start chanting that I should stay. I tell them that I'm on a mission and have to go, and they look at me as if I've broken their hearts.

"Please, try to understand," I beg.

"Okay, then why don't you come and play with us, just for a little while?" Stephanie says.

I look at the stopwatch; I have eight minutes left. "Okay, I can play, but only for a bit," I reply. They cheer and come sit at the base of the tree with us. I talk and play. It's so much fun; I am rolling on the ground.

"This is awesome, but I have to go," I tell them.

"Go?" Stephanie says. "You're not going anywhere. You're staying with us—forever."

I panic and try to get up from the ground, but they are holding me back. All the kids are pulling me toward the base of the tree.

"Stephanie, let me go!"

"Never! You belong with us!" She cackles, and as her laughter hits the air, her hold on me tightens. I turn my head around to plead with her face to face.

But when I turn, I don't see Stephanie or any of the kids. Instead, I come face to face with a massive serpent. There were never any kids. The snakes just tricked me. The whole time I was playing around, I was really in a den of snakes. They are coiling themselves around me. They're going to squeeze me to death!

I try as hard as I can to wiggle free, but the more I try, the tighter the snakes squeeze me. I force myself to stop panicking. That's not going to help at all. I remember Madam Monday telling me to be clever.

Think, Gabrielle, think! The forest is specific to you. Why are your friends squeezing you? They're not. They would never do that. I am. I am squeezing myself. I am controlling the snakes, not the other way around.

"No one can hold me back but me," I say. The snakes encircle my neck, and just before I pass out, I shout, "Let me go, now!" And just like that, the snakes turn into dried-up tree branches and fall to the ground. I am free.

I take a few seconds to catch my breath, but not too long. I look at the stopwatch, and I am down to five minutes. I start running through the forest, desperately searching for the next task that will lead me to the snail. I come to a large, dark tunnel. There's a message carved into the side of the tunnel: "Cave of Echoes."

I'm not sure what's in there, but I don't want to go inside. In fact, I think it's best to get as far away from the cave as possible. I turn to try to go around and make my own path, but I feel something sting me on my neck.

I try to yell, "Ouch!" but no sound comes out of my mouth.

I look up to see what has bitten me; it's a glow-in-the-dark bee. I've never seen a bee like that. And I've been stung by bees before. This felt much worse. I moan in pain, but again, no sound comes out.

Did I lose my voice?

I try to talk, sing, or shout. But nothing happens. Yup, my voice is gone. I look at the bee hovering over me. It stole my voice.

I chase it around hoping, but it's a fast little pest. I try to swat at it, but it dodges me and dives into the cave. So much for avoiding the dark hole.

The cave has the stench of decay. Rodents sweep across my feet as I enter. The only light is daylight, and the deeper inside the cave I get, the less light there is. I really don't want to keep going. I hear strange animal sounds and feel movement all around me. The last thing I want to do is keep going deeper inside the cave, but I need my voice.

The last drop of daylight is fading from the depths of the cave. Everything in me wants to run out, but I remind myself to focus on finding the bee. Something swoops down from the roof of the cave and cuts through the air. I can just make out its shadowy form—a bat!

Bats! Really? Argh!

I manage to wave it away, but I don't know if there are more on the ceiling. Luckily, I spot the glowing bee as it flies toward the corner of the cave. I follow just in time to watch it land—in the nest of sleeping bats!

I look around for something to catch the bee before it flies away. I take out the clear tube Madam Monday gave me to contain the snail. I climb onto a large stone and reach as far as I can. I am only inches away from the bee. All I have to do is trap it under the vial without waking up the bats.

I've almost got it; I just need one more inch—but I tumble off the rock and down to the ground. That spooks the bee and wakes the bats—all the bats. The cave is flooded with the wild creatures. They fly angrily toward me as they try to bite my flesh off. I fight them off with everything I have. I don't care how much it hurts; I won't leave this stupid cave without my voice.

I spot the bee glowing just below my knee. It's flying in circles, having a good time. I reach for the tube I dropped when I fell, and just as the bee is about to soar high in the sky again, I trap it between my palm and the clear vial. I take off running toward the exit as the bats swarm overhead.

I make it out to the daylight, take cover behind a tree, and shield my face and head with my arms. I'm still holding the bee in my palm, and it's stinging me in protest. Finally, the bats fly off, and now it's just the bee and me.

I bring the clear vial up to my face. I can't speak, but it

knows exactly what I want. The bee has an attitude. It turns its back on me. I show it a stern expression, the one my mom shows when I won't go to bed. Finally, the bee dims its light. The light forms a small glowing circle. I open the clear vial, and the ball of light comes close to my face. It sinks into my throat and my voice returns. The bee takes off into the air.

"I have a voice! I have a voice!" I shout gleefully. My voice echoes throughout the forest. I look at the stopwatch—I only have two minutes left! Oh no! I have to hurry, or I'll be stuck here forever.

I'm bruised all over and have a bunch of cuts thanks to my fight with the bats. My body hurts from falling on the ground of the cave, and my right arm is bleeding. I don't dare to even stop and treat my wounds. There just isn't enough time. I have to find the last task. But what is it? All I see here are trees, in every direction. What's the final task?

Something roars so loudly that it causes the ground beneath me to shake. It sounds like . . . No, it can't be. I turn and come eye to eye with a mammoth jaguar. It's stark white, with icy blue eyes and jagged fangs. It opens its gaping jaw and roars again. I look to my left. Another one appears. I dare look to my right and see one more jaguar; there's three of them and only one of me.

"Um . . . any chance you guys are friendly?" They all growl and take off after me. I run through the woods as fast as I can. The tree branches cut through my skin as the wind howls in my ears. My heart is jumping so much that it almost finds its way out of my body. The adrenaline pumping through me makes my whole body shiver. I run and run until I come to the edge of a cliff. It's a big chasm. There is no way to get to the other side. And below is raging sea and certain death.

"How am I gonna get to the other side?" I shout at the forest, as if expecting it to reply.

Out of nowhere, a bridge appears. It's missing pieces and looks like it could fall apart at any moment. There are two words written on the wooden steps: "Speak truth."

I hear the jaguars' roars behind me. They are coming. I leap onto the bridge just as the animals burst through the forest. I land too hard on the fragile panel, and it splits apart under my feet. I'm falling quickly, plunging to the dark waters below. I remember the two words on the steps.

"I'm afraid," I shout. And suddenly, a panel appears under my feet. It stops my fall.

"I've made a mistake. But I'm a good person. I'm trying." Three additional panels appear. Soon, an entire bridge forms, allowing me get to the other side. The animals are gone. And although I'm pretty bruised and freaked out, I'm alive. And I have ten seconds to find the snail. I look high and low for the creature but can't find it. I hate to say it, but I may have failed.

No! You will not fail. You are from a strong family that has endured many painful things. You don't get to fail, Gabrielle!

"Argh!" I shout into the sky as I lean on the base of the tree nearby. I look at the stopwatch. I have five seconds.

Okay, keep looking.

Four seconds.

I search the ground, the tree, and under the rocks.

Three seconds.

Something tickles my shoulder. I shoo it away.

Two seconds.

Something feels slimy on my shoulder.

"What's on me?" I shout, frustrated. I look on my shoulder—it's a snail. No—it's *the* snail! I can tell by its rainbow-striped shell.

"Gotcha!" I shout as I grab the snail just as the stopwatch goes off.

Time's up! The light grows bright, so bright that I have to shield my eyes. When I open my eyes again, I'm back in Madam Monday's home, with my friends! I hold out the snail and put it in the vial.

"You did it!" Carmen says. We all cheer, and I try to catch my breath. Madam Monday comes over with bottles filled with an oddly colored liquid.

"What is that?" I ask.

"These mixtures will heal you," she says. "Come, let me apply them to your skin. What happened in there? You look like you were fighting an army!"

"Well, an army of jaguars and bats," I reply. Carmen is shocked. I put the vial down on the table and start to explain all the things that happened in the forest as Madam Monday treats my cuts.

"No, stop!" Madam Monday shouts suddenly toward the window. We follow her gaze and watch as Rocky runs down the side of the building with our snail.

"Rocky, bring that back! Where are you going?" I shout.

"I made a deal with Lady Lydia. If I bring her this snail, she'll change me into a rabbit!"

"No! You can't!" I cry.

"Sorry, guys," he says. Carmen and I watch in horror as Rocky runs away with our only hope to save my family.

CHAPTER SEVENTEEN
Friends Like You

WE LOOK FOR ROCKY for the next hour, and he's nowhere to be found. We even go to the park to see if he's lurking around there. We come back to Madam Monday's house looking almost as bad as we feel.

"I hate to pile on, but Lydia sent you a message," Madam Monday says. She points us toward the writing literally on the wall. It says:

> *If you want to see your family again,*
> *come to the park at midnight.*
> *Ready to make a wish.*

"She needs to meet tonight because tonight is a full super-moon. That means the moon is at the point in its orbit closest to the earth, and it appears bigger in the sky," Madam Monday says. "Doing it tonight would allow her unimaginable powers. She will use them to complete her plan to make everyone act, look, and think the same. There will be no more culture or diversity anywhere. You need to stop her before the moon is directly overhead, at midnight."

"We can't go without the snail. We won't have a way to free the kids in the stream," Carmen says.

"I know, but I have to meet her," I say. "She has my family. If I don't go to the park at midnight, there's no telling what she'll do."

"Any luck finding Rocky?" Madam Monday asks.

"Nope." Carmen sighs.

"He's gone. We don't know where," I admit.

"All this time Rocky's been working for Lady Lydia? How could he do this to us?" Carmen asks.

"It's my fault. I should have known that the witch would have spies. All this time he was pretending to be our friend," I mumble.

Madam Monday pours us two glasses of milk and places a plate of double chocolate chip cookies in front of us. We take the food, but we don't eat.

"Now, girls, there's no need to look so devastated," Madam Monday says.

"But Rocky lied to us," I say. "He tricked us into thinking he was our friend. And we fell for it. We fell for the whole act!"

"I have a feeling Rocky hasn't had a lot of friends in his life," Madam Monday replies. "He made this deal with Lydia so that he could be loved and wanted. He thought he could do that as a rabbit. But then he found you two. And you loved him for who he was. You didn't ask that he be someone else. That's called acceptance. And it's a wonderful gift to give to someone. I have a feeling Rocky wasn't expecting to love you all so much. But he does. And maybe, in the end, he'll do the right thing."

"But what if he doesn't? Now how will we stop Lady Lydia?" I ask.

"Witch law forbids me from getting in the way, since the deal that was made is between you and Lydia. But I can arm you with what I have. This might help."

She waves her hand and creates musical notes in the air. We do as she orders and watch as the notes seep into the radio on the counter.

"What was that?" Carmen says.

"That's called a slumber song," Madam Monday replies. "It can put the most powerful of beings to sleep."

"So we play it for Lady Lydia, and she falls asleep?" Carmen asks.

"Yes—although the more powerful she is, the harder it will be to keep her asleep."

"Won't we fall asleep too?" I ask.

"No. The song only works on witches. So as soon as she drifts off, you have to tie her up. Then find the vial with the snail to set the other kids in the stream free."

"But after Rocky gives her the vial with the snail, won't she destroy it?" I ask.

"No, not Lydia. She'll keep the vial close because she can use it later, should another witch challenge her. Also, she won't trust anyone with it. She'll most likely carry it with her."

"So the song will put her to sleep, and then we try to take the vial off her. Got it," Carmen says.

"If you can free the kids in the stream, that might free your family too," Madam Monday says. "And if not, it will at the very least make Lydia weak enough to force her to tell you where she's keeping them."

"We can do it. We just need to trick Lady Lydia into letting us play the song," I tell myself. Then Madam Monday hands over the only book ever written about Lady Lydia.

"We're not going to be able to learn all this info about Lady Lydia before our meeting tonight," I tell her.

"No, but just keep these two things in mind: one, there is no point in trying to run away from her, because you made the deal. And no human on earth has been able to stop Lady Lydia from collecting what was owed to her."

"So no running away. Got it. What's the second thing?" Carmen asks.

"This is the most important thing of all: remember that while you don't have magic, you have something just as good —your words. And words can be uplifting," Madam Monday says as she looks deep into our eyes. "Repeat it after me— words can be uplifting." We repeat it.

A few hours later, we head to Carmen's place to get ready for midnight. We need to go over the plan as if our lives depend on it, because . . . mine does.

When we enter Carmen's apartment, it's quiet. She tells me that her family is out running last-minute errands for

Gloria's birthday. Her mom left us food, but again, we aren't really in the mood to eat. We are waiting for midnight so we can go meet the witch.

"Do you think Rocky liked us, or was it all a lie?" I ask as we plop down on Carmen's bed.

"I don't know. He's so cute! How can something so tiny be so tricky?"

"I thought we were friends . . . I thought . . ." I bury my face in my hands. Carmen puts her head on my shoulder. "That's it. I'm never trusting anyone again."

"Even if that someone is adorable and very sorry?" someone asks. We look toward the window and see Rocky. He presses his sad face into the glass.

"What are you doing here? Haven't you hurt us enough already? Thanks to you, I may never see my family!" I bark at him.

"I know. I'm so sorry," he says.

"That's not good enough. How could you betray us?" I demand.

"I made a deal with the witch before I knew you two. I had no idea how awesome you guys would be. Anyway, I never had friends before. And I thought I could get them if I looked like a rabbit."

"So why aren't you a rabbit?" Carmen asks.

"I gave the vial to Lady Lydia, and she said she'll make me a rabbit after you make your last wish," Rocky says.

"Well, that's not gonna happen. So you're out of luck!" Carmen says.

"I don't care about that anymore. When I left Madam Monday's place, I felt terrible. You two were so nice to me, and I hurt you. I made a mistake. I don't want to be a rabbit anymore. I want friends—friends like you. Can you ever forgive me?"

Carmen and I look at each other. She says to Rocky, "How can we trust you after everything?"

He thinks for a minute. "I'll tell you everything you need to know about the meeting tonight. And the witch still thinks I'm on her side, so we can use that."

"Are you really sorry? Can we really trust you?" I ask.

"Yes. I've never had friends before. I don't want to lose you two," he says as his head falls.

"Okay, but you have to help us get her," I reply.

"Really? I'm back in?" Rocky asks.

"We've all made mistakes. You're back in—if you promise no more secret alliances with witches," Carmen says as she opens the window.

Rocky starts to dance and says, "Yes, I promise."

As soon as he enters the room, he jumps up on Carmen's bed and shouts, "The band is back together!"

———

We make our way down the dimly lit path that leads to the bridge, and although it's summer now, a chill clings to the air. I can't help but feel like we are being watched. It could be my imagination, but I swear the tree branches are following us; the birds are tracking our every move. And is it possible that even the stars above our heads are reporting to Lady Lydia?

I ask my friends, "Does anyone else feel like . . ."

"Like we're not alone?" Carmen finishes.

"Exactly," I reply.

We walk the rest of the way in silence, going over the plan in our heads. When we get under the bridge, we see Lady Lydia standing in front of the stream. She's wearing a long, reddish cape made entirely of fire ants. Her blood-red nail polish and lipstick gleam in the moonlight. And Madam Monday was right: she is wearing the glass vial around her neck, with the snail in it. It's still alive.

Lady Lydia eyes us with anticipation. She rubs her hands together and smirks. She motions for us to come closer. I can almost feel the excitement bouncing off her.

"I see you brought an audience," Lady Lydia says.

"After I make my third wish, my essence will be trapped with you, so this is my only chance to say goodbye to my friend," I reply.

Lady Lydia looks over at Rocky.

"I mean say goodbye to my real friends," I shout at him.

Lady Lydia laughs and says there are no such things as friends.

"That's not true! Carmen is my friend. And I have plenty of friends back in Haiti."

"Yes, the friends you were so willing to forget about to embrace your new culture," she says.

I lower my head.

"She made a mistake. She knows better now. And that's okay. People make mistakes," Carmen says.

"Well, I don't," Lady Lydia says. "I plan things to the bitter end. I worked out every single detail of this day. Now, make your third wish so I can collect the last essence I need to make Brooklyn perfect!"

"Lady Lydia, we can't all be the same. If we're all the same, then we lose ourselves. Don't you see that?" I plead.

"You children are fools! I'm here to ensure perfection and harmony. That only happens when there is nothing different or unique in the world. Now I've waited too long for this. Make the wish, or I'll end your family!" she says as she waves her arms and opens up a portal in the middle of the park. I see my family inside the portal. They look terrified and confused. I run over to the portal, but Lady Lydia closes it up.

"Hey, bring them back!" I demand.

"Is that your wish? Are you making a wish?" she asks eagerly.

"No—no, I'm not. Not yet."

"Well, that's too bad, because I'm surely going to take them now!" she says as she waves her hand and makes the portal reappear. She summons white smoke in the shape of a dragon. It flies into the portal and surrounds my family.

"Make the wish, or else . . ." she threatens.

"Okay. I'll make my last wish," I reply.

"Finally! Perfection will be mine!" She cackles as she makes the dragon disappear.

I look at Carmen, who nods. "I need one thing before I make my last wish," I inform Lady Lydia.

"And what is that?" she asks.

"A dance," I reply.

"What dance?"

"In Haiti, we have a dance to say goodbye to earth. And since, after my wish, I will be trapped in the stream, I'd like to do the dance to say goodbye to earth."

"I've never heard of such a thing," Lady Lydia says suspiciously.

"It's true!" Carmen adds quickly. "We have that kind of dance in Mexico, too. It's to thank the land for everything it gave us."

Rocky leans in and whispers in the witch's ear, "I've heard of that. It's a real thing. Just let them dance, and then you can have everything you've always wanted."

"How long is this dance?" Lady Lydia asks. "The moon is nearly overhead. You have to make your wish by then."

"It will only take a few moments," I reply. "Please, let me say goodbye to the earth that kept me alive up until now."

"Argh, fine! But hurry up!" Lady Lydia says.

I nod at Carmen; she takes the radio out of her backpack and starts to play the slumber song. Carmen and I begin to dance. It's nothing that's ever been done before. We make it up as we go along. We mix and match all kinds of dances to the smooth, relaxing sound coming from the radio. The song is doing exactly what Madam Monday said it would do: it's making Lady Lydia sleepy.

She's watching the movements closely, and her eyelids are drooping as she moves her head to the music. Carmen and I get close enough to the vial, but the witch isn't sleepy enough to let us take it. We surround her, still dancing. She watches us as she gets sleepier and sleepier.

"The song . . . Something's wrong . . . The song . . . It's making me . . ." She starts to walk toward us, stumbles forward, and falls flat on her face. The whole park can hear her snoring.

"Rocky, now!" I whisper. He jumps on top of Lady Lydia and yanks the vial off her neck. He tosses it to me, but it falls to the ground and starts to roll away. Carmen chases it while Rocky and I tie the witch's feet together. Thankfully, because she's asleep, so is her army of fire ants.

"Hurry!" Rocky says. Carmen comes back to us looking frazzled. Rocky and I exchange a quick look of panic.

"Carmen, where is the vial?" I ask.

"Egg has it," she says.

"Who?" Rocky and I ask at the same time.

"Egg—he's a pit bull. He was playing fetch with his owner and he saw the vial and took off after it."

"What? He ate the vial with the snail?" I ask.

"No, but he thinks it's a toy. He's playing with it."

"We have to get that vial before Lady Lydia wakes up!"

"I'm on it!" Rocky says.

"Rocky, it's a big dog," Carmen says. "I don't think you can—"

"No, Carmen, I will do this. You guys were my friends, and I let you down. I want to make it up to you. I'm on it!"

Carmen shows him the direction the dog took, and Rocky takes off running.

"Is she tied up tight?" Carmen asks, looking at Lady Lydia.

"As tight as I could get it," I reply nervously.

"How much longer do we have until she wakes up?" Carmen asks.

"Not long at all, fools!" Lady Lydia yells as she springs up and uses her magic to free herself. She hovers angrily in the air and glares at us. "I see you had help from Monday. Well, it wasn't enough. Nothing you do can stop this from happening!"

As she is ranting and raving, Rocky appears behind her. He shouts, "Egg, attack!" And out of nowhere, a pit bull jumps into the air and pounces on the witch.

"Gabrielle, the moon! Here!" Rocky hands me the vial. We only have one chance to get the snail into the water. Lady Lydia will break free from Egg's jaws at any moment.

"Go, Gabrielle! Go!" Carmen shouts as I run to the water's edge. I uncap the vial just as Lady Lydia breaks free from the dog.

"No!" she says behind me. She summons the sky to open and brings down thunder and lightning, each bolt only inches from me. She orders the lightning to strike as close to the edge of the water as possible so that I can't get anywhere near it.

"Gabrielle, the lightning—it's gonna get you if you go any closer," Rocky shouts.

"I have to try," I reply as I take a deep breath and run toward the water. I finally get close enough to drop the snail into the stream. As soon as the snail hits the water, the stream parts and a slew of spirits leap from the depths of the water and up into the air.

They fly high above our heads and enter the light of the moon. Every essence that escapes leaves Lady Lydia weaker and weaker. She's now too weak to stand. She's on the ground moaning. The lightning has stopped. She doesn't have enough power left to summon anything in the sky anymore.

"No, my collection! No!" the witch says.

All the essences that were trapped in the stream are now free, the stream closes back up, and the surface of the water is still.

It's over. We won.

"It was going to be perfection! I was going to give Brooklyn perfection!" she cries.

"She's weak now; she can't harness enough power to keep hiding my family. So, where are they? Where's my family?" I ask. I look around for them. They should be right here. The three of us look all over the place, but there's no sign of them.

Suddenly, the defeated witch on the ground begins to laugh. It's a chilling laugh, the kind that makes you feel cold inside, that makes its way down your spine.

"You may have robbed me of my dream world, but you won't get what you want," she says.

"Where are they? What did you do to them, witch?" I shout.

"You better tell us, or we'll sic Egg on you again, and this time, he'll finish you off!" Carmen says.

"Start talking, lady!" Rocky adds.

She's weak, too weak to stand up. Yet she's found something to laugh about, and that worries us. Could it be that she's actually already done away with my family?

"Lady Lydia, talk!" I roar.

"You see, dear, the deal I made with you was a fair one. I told you the rules, and we made the deal in good faith. When you put that snail in the water, it did weaken me. In fact, I can't summon a butterfly, let alone enough magic to overpower you three. But I have a feeling I will get some power back very soon."

"And who's going to give it to you?" I ask.

"You are. Your essence is stronger than any of the kids I was holding captive in the stream. Just one drop of your essence can power me up. So go ahead. Make your third wish. And while I won't be able to change Brooklyn into the perfect world, I will take you as my consolation prize."

"What are you talking about? We beat you!" I reply.

"Yes, you foiled my plans. Good for you. But that won't bring your family back. If you want them to return, alive and well, you will need to wish it. And when you do, you will be mine. I will trap you in that stream, and since the snail is only useful once, there is no getting out for you."

"No, Gabrielle, don't listen to her. You can't make that wish," Carmen says.

"She's right. Wishing it is the only way to bring them back," I say.

"Yes, but then you'll belong to her forever," Carmen says.

"I know. But it's my family's freedom or mine. And I'm the reason this happened. I love them, and I owe it to them to make sure they are safe."

"Even if it means the end for you?" Rocky says.

"Yes," I reply softly.

"But we can't let the witch win," Carmen argues.

"She's not winning. She'll never be able to collect essences again. Her time is over."

"But I will still get to keep you captive." Lady Lydia laughs.

"Yeah, you will. But all that matters is my family," I reply.

I look at my friends, and tears spring to my eyes. They aren't tears of sadness; they are tears of joy. "I finally feel like I belong here. And it's not because of magic. It's because I have friends like you two. Thank you. Please look after my family."

"Aw, so sad," the witch says.

"Be quiet, witch!" Rocky says.

"Don't worry—when you make the wish, you'll have until noon today to say goodbye to all your friends."

"Why would you give me that chance?" I ask.

"It's not me. It's the rule. You get to say goodbye. But at noon, I come for you," Lady Lydia says.

"Okay, let's do it," I say.

"Gabrielle . . ." Carmen says.

"It's what I have to do," I tell her and Rocky. They nod and begin to tear up. The witch stands up and hands me the box with the last mango slice. I take the mango in my hand.

"You guys get out of here. I don't want her coming for any of you," I tell them. Rocky and Carmen reluctantly flee. Now, it's just the witch and me.

"I wish for my aunt, uncle, and cousins to come back to me, safe and unharmed. Right here and right now," I say, and put the final slice of mango into my mouth.

A portal appears and spits out my family. I run up to them and hug them as tightly as I possibly can. Rocky stands near and tells me what they are saying.

"Gabrielle, it's too late to be out here. Let's go home. Soccer rematch this weekend. Okay?" Rocky translates for my uncle.

I look at him sadly and reply in English, "Okay, Uncle."

"I'm thinking rice and beans for dinner. Maybe some fried pork or goat? What do you think?" my aunt asks.

"Sounds good."

The twins play with my hair, and Kayla says she can't be seen here because she isn't wearing the proper "park" outfit. I laugh at her and hug her. She has no idea why I'm being emotional.

"Hey, there's a strange lady behind you," my uncle says. I turn to face Lady Lydia.

"Is she a friend of yours?" my aunt asks.

"No, she's not," I reply.

"Yes, but we will have more than enough time to get to know each other," Lady Lydia says. "Because in a few hours, you'll be mine . . . forever!"

CHAPTER EIGHTEEN
American

I LOOK AT MY WATCH for the hundredth time—it's almost noon. Our principal, Mr. Moore, is at the podium, and his speech is so boring that even the teachers are nodding off.

"It's important that you all remember: keeping the school clean means you care. So, let's make sure we all care . . ." He then goes on and on about lateness and the importance of filling out permission slips for class trips.

"You students must be responsible. It's not fun for your principal to field a hundred calls from your parents because you forgot your field trip permission slips at home. Sometimes your principal is busy in his office, busy doing principal things."

"Watching soap operas!" some kid yells out. Everyone laughs.

"That's an outrageous lie! Now . . . sometimes on my lunch breaks I might tune into *All My Children* to see if Angie and Jesse have finally united. Those two have so much going for them. Why must they be torn apart? Why is love so cruel?"

Mr. Moore is tearing up as he looks off into the distance. Ms. King—the assistant principal—elbows him in the ribs.

"Ah yes, where was I? Oh—yes, responsibility. Let's really think about this: What is responsibility?"

The kids groan and roll their eyes. Thankfully, Ms. King politely cuts him off and tells the kids to give him a big round of applause. A few kids clap, but most don't.

"Come on now, you kids can do better," Ms. King says. The kids clap again, this time louder. The clapping starts to fade into the background as I look at the time: 11:40. Soon, it will all be over. I will be Lady Lydia's prisoner forever.

"This is crazy," Carmen says. "We shouldn't be here. If you can dodge the witch for twenty-four hours, she can't touch you. So all we have to do is keep you hidden for a day."

I smile sadly. "We both know that wherever I am on earth, the witch will find me. And anyway, I want to be here for Culture Day. I need to make up for what I did."

Suddenly I hear a hum. It's low, but it's getting louder with every passing moment. The hum is coming from inside the walls of the auditorium.

Rocky jumps on my lap. "We should get you outta here! Fast!"

"Rocky, remember what the book said: 'There is nowhere on earth anyone can run from the witch,'" I remind him.

Rocky turns to Carmen and begs her, "Make Gabrielle go before it's too late."

"Rocky's right," Carmen says. "We should get you to safety."

"I'm the third in line to speak," I say. "I have to wait for my turn to go up there. If this is my last day of freedom, I have to talk about Haiti. I owe that to my family."

"And now, our first Culture Day presenter—Connor Long!" Ms. King announces. Connor pops up out of his seat. He has big glasses and walks like a proud peacock. He marches up to the stage wearing a kilt and holding bagpipes. He gets onto the stage and begins his presentation.

We don't hear what Connor has to say; we can't. I'm too busy looking at the giant creatures burrowing out from the walls. I hold on to the armrest so hard my hands shake. They are here: FEAR.

The creatures are terrifying. They are massive blood-red spiders, with scorpion tails and unhinged jaws. Their spiked claws snap at the air as they dig out of the walls. Their red and gold wings flap wildly as they emerge. I think only the three of us can see them, because everyone else is calm and watching the stage.

The Flying Evil Army of Rage is getting into position. There were three of them, but by the time Connor finishes playing his bagpipes, there are six. Soon, FEAR grows. Now there are dozens of them crawling up along the walls, the floor, and the ceiling.

"Don't worry, guys. They aren't after you; they are after me," I remind my friends.

"That's not making me feel better," Carmen says as the army multiplies.

"Yeah, same here," Rocky adds.

Connor finishes his presentation. The kids clap. The army grows. The three of us hold hands. We're all terrified, but at least we're together.

"And now, for our second presentation—Johnny Douglas, come to the stage."

Johnny makes his way to the stage wearing a soccer jersey. He's really popular, and the kids cheer as he approaches the podium.

The humming from the army gets louder. It's now 11:55. And in five minutes, the witch will come, and her army will take me away forever.

"Are you sure you don't want to run away?" Carmen says. "I have a cousin in Mexico who makes costumes for movies. She could make you a good disguise. Lady Lydia would never find you."

"Thanks, but I've been running away for too long," I reply. It's hard to hear her over the humming and the sound of my heart pounding against my chest.

"There has to be something we can do. Something we missed," Carmen says. "The book says no one on earth can stop the witch. And when we went to see Madam Monday, she said to remember to use our voices for good and that words are uplifting. So if we put that together, what do we have? What does it all mean?"

"I don't think there's time to figure it out. Look!" I point as FEAR gets into formation to create an archway in the auditorium wall. They are making way for their leader—Lady Lydia.

"Don't look over there. Stay focused, Gabrielle. What are we missing? How do we get you away from the witch?"

"Okay, we have five minutes," I say. "You guys keep thinking, while I give my presentation."

"What if we don't solve the problem in time?" Carmen says.

I hug her really hard. "Then at least my last few moments of freedom were spent with my friends." She hugs me back.

Rocky joins us and takes out a handkerchief. "Why her? Why, oh why?" Rocky says as he blows his nose into his handkerchief.

Johnny finishes his presentation. The kids clap at the exact time that lightning hits the window. The army welcomes its evil witch leader—Lady Lydia. She's wearing a liquid cape made of tears. I know because I can hear the cloth sobbing. Her long black and red dress is made of blood-soaked fangs and flows behind her. Her eyes are alive with malice and wickedness.

"Hello, dear. I believe you have something of mine—oh yes, your essence!" she says as she makes her way toward me. Rocky and Carmen never let go of my hands. The witch laughs. "Are they supposed to stop me from getting to you?"

"We won't let you hurt Gabrielle!" Carmen says.

"Yeah, that's right, not on our watch! Put 'em up," Rocky says.

The witch waves her hand, and both Rocky and Carmen go flying across the room.

"No!" I shout as I race to make sure they are okay. No one

in the auditorium can see what's going on. It's just us, on our own.

"Are you guys okay?" I ask.

They nod. I help them both stand up. Lady Lydia gets ready to attack them again. "Don't you dare, witch! Your business is with me, not them. Come and get me." I ball my hands into fists and place them firmly at my sides.

"My dear, I'll feast on your essence until nothing remains," Lady Lydia says. "You'll spend the rest of your life trapped in my stream! It's time, dear. Say goodbye to your freedom. You belong to me!"

"Not yet I don't!" I point to the clock on the wall at the back of the auditorium. "I still have four minutes before noon."

"Four minutes, ha! What can you do in four minutes?"

"I can make things right," I reply as I march toward the stage.

"And now, our third and final presenter—born and raised right here in America—Gabrielle Jean." All the kids clap for me. I look over at Rocky and Carmen for what will be the last time. I nod and try to put on my best smile. It doesn't turn out so well. It's a sad smile, but when you have true friends, you don't have to pretend to be happy when you're not.

"Gabrielle, come on up!" Ms. King says.

I make my way near the edge of the stage; Mrs. Bartell stands in front of me. I can tell from the look on her face that she sees FEAR too. She knows the witch is here. Tears fall from her eyes.

"I'm sorry that I didn't listen to you," I tell her.

She hugs me and says, "I'm proud of you. You're a special girl. There's no one on earth like you."

I thank her and head toward the podium. Carmen and Rocky follow me. The map is already on the stage, along with the photos I picked to be pinned to it. Some of them are pictures of my family; some are of Stephanie and my other friends. There are also pictures of my village and my favorite mango tree. I hold on to the podium and look out at everyone.

"Hello . . . I have something to confess."

Everyone goes quiet. The witch points to the clock and smiles. My hands are ice cold, and my knees feel like they will give out at any moment.

"Gabrielle, you can do this," Mrs. Bartell says. My throat is drier than the desert. The humming has stopped, and now the auditorium is too quiet. Lady Lydia is enjoying how nervous I am. But I'll show her!

"What I want to say is . . . I'm not from America. I wasn't born here. I was born in a country called Haiti."

All the kids gasp and start muttering to each other. I'm really nervous about continuing, because it's time to tell the truth.

"Gabrielle, you can do it," Rocky says.

"Just think really hard about back home. When I miss my family in Mexico, I think of one thing I love and then I feel like I'm there. Just try, Gabrielle. Think of one thing . . ." Carmen whispers to me.

I hear laughter, but I'm not sure where it's coming from. I smell wet earth and feel drops of water on my skin.

"Rain. I love it when it rains . . ." I reply. And just like that, all my memories of Haiti come flooding back. I hear the laughter as we run like crazy through the village.

I clear my throat and keep going. "Sometimes in Haiti, we don't have enough food to eat. Sometimes we don't even have enough water to drink. When I came here, I was embarrassed about all the things Haiti didn't have. So I pretended I was born here instead. But that was stupid, because there are a lot of good things about Haiti too.

"When I was little, my mom would balance the world on her back, our groceries on her head, and me on her hip. She'd carry that load for miles in the hot sun. She never stopped, even when she was tired. The moms in Haiti are strong and tough. They are superheroes.

"When my stomach hurt from hunger, my dad would tell us jokes. Sometimes he'd make my mom and me laugh so much we'd forget we were sad, forget we were hungry. His laugh is more healing than medicine; it's magic. Dads in Haiti are magic.

"Haitians use spiritual songs, stories, and humor as a weapon against hopelessness. They slay problems the size of dragons and conquer their fears by being resourceful, being strong. The people of Haiti are strong. I came here, and I forgot about that. And that was unfair to them.

"My country taught me to be strong, courageous, and resourceful. I gave all that up. I gave up my native language, my culture, and my family so I could have new friends. But real friends help you celebrate who you are, not hide it." I look over at Carmen and Rocky; they smile at me.

"There's another reason why I tried to hide being Haitian. I thought it was the only way I could be an American. Being in America means I have a chance to reach my dreams, but if it weren't for Haiti, I'd never even know how to dream." I feel the tears well up in my eyes. I hold on tighter to the podium. There's a big lump in my throat. The more I try to fight my feelings, the harder they are to control.

"I'm sorry I lied to everyone about who I am. I was ashamed, but not anymore. I know it looks like I stand here alone, but the truth is, I'm not alone. I carry my family, my culture, and my history with me everywhere I go." I take a deep breath, and suddenly, I see them in my head: my parents, Stephanie, the village. All the things that help make me who I am. They're smiling at me.

"When I first came to school, people teased me and said mean things. I should not have listened to them, because they don't really know about my homeland. They see it on TV sometimes, and it looks small and weak. But Haiti is much more than what you see on TV.

"Just like what my friend Carmen told me once about her homeland, Mexico. It's a place she loves because it's where her family and her heart live. She's proud of it. She didn't let anyone take that pride away. I did, but not anymore. I'm taking my dignity back. I come from the land of superheroes, magicians, and warriors. I come from Haiti.

"I'm also proud that I live in America now; this country lets me hold on to both my native land and my new home. I hope America always stays that way. My name is Gabrielle Jean. I am a proud Haitian. I am a proud American."

The first person to jump up and start cheering is Mrs. Bartell. And then Carmen, and Rocky. And soon, the others join in. In fact, I get a standing ovation!

"Wow, great job, Gabrielle!" Ms. King says. "How on earth did you think of that? Your words were so inspirational. So uplifting!"

As soon as she says that to me, it hits me like lightning! Carmen and I turn to each other and shout at the same time, "I got it!"

Carmen says, "Earth! That's it, Gabrielle! No one on earth can stop the witch, but if you're up in the air, you aren't touching the earth at all!"

"Yes, that's right!" Rocky says. "But how do we stop you from touching the earth?"

"I know how," I reply just as the clock strikes noon. I run to the microphone. I look out the window. The witch has split the sky apart with red lightning. The school building begins to shake.

"Everyone, if you tell the truth about who you are, if you are proud to be from wherever you're from, stand up and tell us. We want to know who you are, who you really are. Your words can uplift us," I shout.

"Oh! She means literally, Rocky!" Carmen says. She runs for the microphone.

Lady Lydia waves her hand again, and the podium is hurled into the air and smashes against the wall. FEAR is on the move, and so is the witch. The end is coming for me. I fight them off as much as I can. They spit their poison-laced web at me, and I barely get out of the way in time. Rocky tries to fend off the creatures as Carmen runs to get to the microphone.

"I was born in Mexico. We gave the world chocolate, tacos, and popcorn. We invented color TV. And aside from Spanish, there are over one hundred different languages spoken in Mexico. My name is Carmen Hernández. I am a proud Mexican. I am a proud American." The words fall out of Carmen's mouth and bend and twist until they become one large feather. It travels through the air and lands on my shoulder blade.

The army is everywhere. And everyone in the auditorium can see FEAR now. Carmen pleads with the auditorium to share their story and be proud of who they are. While I try to fend off the army, I hear Mrs. Bartell's voice come over the microphone. She talks about her love for Haiti. Her words grow into a feather, just like Carmen's. Soon, others join her.

"My family is Muslim. We're from Turkey. I wear a hijab. It's a part of my faith. We believe in peace. My dad sings off-key in the shower; my sister steals the remote when I'm not looking. And my mom lets me sample dessert before it gets to the table. My name is Afra Asad. I am a proud Muslim. I am a proud American."

"I'm not from Japan. I'm not from China. Both places are

nice, but that's not where I'm from. We're from Thailand. That's in Southeast Asia. My grandfather is an artist, my mom is a mechanic, and no one in the house break-dances better than me! My name is Gan Wu. I am a proud Thai. I am a proud American."

All the students begin to talk at once. They don't even need a microphone. They are yelling out their stories. Before I know it, feathers are flying across the room, from every direction, all headed for me. They land on my back and arrange themselves to make a pair of glorious wings!

Lady Lydia is livid. "No! She's mine!" she says as she gets up in the air and tries to pull me down. Her army tries to latch on too.

"My name is Rocky! I am a rat!" Rocky says as he jumps off one of the tables and bites the creature's tail. Rocky's words create another feather, letting me hover a few feet in the air.

"I'm Principal Moore, and I love soap operas!"

I hover a little higher, but not high enough to escape the witch's claws. "I can't get away! The wings aren't strong enough. There has to be someone else, someone whose voice has not been heard," I tell Carmen. We both look around and try to figure out whose voice we can add.

"It's me. My voice is missing."

We all turn to follow the sound of Tianna's voice. Uh-oh. This might turn out badly. She looks at me and then at the witch. I can't tell what she's thinking.

"I'm Tianna Thompson. I'm from a place just like Haiti. It's small, and sometimes we don't have much. But we are always happy. My grandfather lets us help him plant bananas and drink juice straight from the coconut. We speak English, but we also speak patois. It's fast, fun, and sounds like music.

"We eat fresh fish by the sea and tell stories. When I came to America, I thought everyone was going to be mean to me, so I had to be mean first. But then I met a girl from Haiti. Haiti isn't too far from Jamaica. We're neighbors. Maybe someday, we might even be friends. I'm Tianna Thompson. I am a proud Jamaican. I am a proud American."

The moment her words fall from her mouth, they bend into feathers nearly twice the size of all the others. They are gold and silver. They cut through the air and head toward me. Lady Lydia whistles and summons a red bolt of lightning. The lightning and the feather both slice through the air at impossible speeds toward me. There's no way to tell which will get to me first. I close my eyes and hold my breath and brace for the end. If this is my last breath, I will take these things with me:

I was loved. I was wanted. By both my old and my new home. By both my old and my new friends. I will face my fate courageously, whether it's red lightning or the feather. I open my eyes.

The feather attaches to my shoulder a fraction of a second before the lightning strike. The gold feather activates all the other ones, and now they are three times as strong. I'm no longer hovering. I'm flying! The wings flap furiously against the air. And when the lightning strikes, it misses me.

The witch moves to call more lightning still, but Mrs.

Bartell trips her, and Lady Lydia falls flat on her face. I watch in horror as she commands her army to attack everyone. FEAR is everywhere!

"Oh no you don't!" I shout from above. I flap my wings as hard as I can as I fly above FEAR and the witch. My massive wings cause a whirlwind.

"Everyone, hold on to something!" I shout. I flap my wings yet again, and a supertornado forms below me. It picks up the witch and her army and sucks them into its void. I wave good-bye as I fly away. The kids below—my friends—wave back. I'm excited and laugh as my wings carry me off.

EPILOGUE

My wings took me far; I flew over all the countries my friends talked about. And when I landed, it was three months later!

I don't have my wings anymore, but I feel like they are still there, should I ever need them again.

I landed a few days before my parents were scheduled to come to America. They finally got the papers they needed to be with me. I'll introduce them to Carmen and my other friends. I'll also show them our class's pet rat—Rocky. He is beloved, and he gets petted all the time. Actually, I think it's gotten to his head. I wanted to talk to him the other day, and I was told I needed to make an appointment!

He's also really good friends with Egg, the dog. The two of them do yoga in the park every Sunday. There's another unlikely friendship—Tianna and me. We're not best friends, but we hang out sometimes, and Carmen comes along too. The more we all get to know each other, the more we find we have in common.

And since I defeated the witch, my Haitian Creole is back! My hair is back the way it was, and, well, I can see what Carmen was talking about. I like my hair the way it was before. I'm teaching Carmen Haitian Creole and she's teaching me Spanish. And I'm also helping Stephanie with her English so she's prepared for the day she comes to America.

"Are you ready?" my uncle asks me.

"Yes!" I reply. The day has finally come. We are here at LaGuardia Airport, waiting to pick up my parents.

"Gabrielle, I see them!" my aunt says.

I look at the crowd of people, and I see them—my parents. I run toward them. My dad picks me up and spins me around. My mom kisses and hugs me—way too tightly.

"Gabrielle! We're so excited to see you. We missed you so much!" she says.

"I missed you too! I have so much to tell you," I reply.

"That's good," my dad says. "We'll need your help. We don't know a lot about America. We don't even speak the language. I'm afraid it will take a long time to learn English."

I smile back at them. "Lucky for you, I know all about how to deal with being new to America. Now, there are a few rules."

My dad smiles. "Oh really? Rules?"

"Yes!" I reply confidently.

"And what are they, Gabrielle?" my mom asks.

"Well, the most important rule is this: If you want a mango, buy one at the store. Don't get one from a witch. She says it's mostly free, but trust me, it'll cost you."